D0868696

THE SUN DOGS OF WINTER

THE ADVENTURES OF DALTON LAIRD

BOOK THREE

A NOVEL BY RUSSELL M. CHACE

TUKONA BOOKS LLC
P.O. Box 447; Cañon City, CO 81215

THE SUN DOGS OF WINTER

A Novel by Russell M. Chace

FOR MORE INFORMATION, CONTACT:

TUKONA BOOKS

P.O. BOX 447

CANON CITY, COLORADO 81215

TRADE PAPERBACK ISBN: 978-1-7330371-4-3

E-BOOK ISBN: 978-1-7330371-5-0

PRINTED IN THE UNITED STATES.

10 9 8 7 6 5 4 3 2 1

FIRST EDITION: MAY 2020

DEDICATION

TO MY WIFE PATRICIA, MY FIRST
CRITIC AND ENCOURAGER.

CHAPTER 1

FRANK WARD HAD CHANGED SOME. Eight years of hard labor in a Canadian prison will do that to a man. Some men change for the better, some for the worse. Ward had changed for the worse. He'd learned to play the system and ended up on a workgang outside the prison walls. Once outside the walls, he killed an officer and made good his escape.

Now, he sat with his back to the wall in the dining area of the Tanana Roadhouse on River Street in Circle City on the Yukon River, just over a hundred miles inside the territorial border of Alaska. Circle City had changed some, too, from what Ward remembered.

Back in '97, Circle was a bustling gold camp, ripe for get-rich-quick schemes. Then, with the discovery of *The Mother Lode* in Canada's Klondike, Circle almost became a ghost town overnight.

Ward drifted with the rush from one town to the next. It'd been several years since Ward

1

had been here. Now, there were abandoned cabins in various stages of decay strewn about the old city. A few miners hung on making a living, but Circle's glory days were over.

Across the table, with his back to the crowd, sat Indian Charlie—a Cree Indian Ward had befriended in prison, and who had helped with Ward's escape.

"Me getting impatient."

Indian Charlie leaned both forearms on the tabletop and inspected the contents of the coffee cup he held in his hands. His comment jerked Ward's mind back to the present.

Ward looked him up and down from under the brim of his hat, pulled low. Charlie always was a little compulsive. Ward had to talk him down a few times in prison, which had averted a few fights. That, in turn, was noticed by the officers and written in their reports, which, in turn played a part in favor of Ward's outside workgang detail.

"Good things come to those who wait," Ward responded. "I've been waitin' and plannin' this for eight long years now. We can handle another day or two."

Ward watched as Charlie took a sip of the strong, black coffee. As Charlie placed the cup back down, he swallowed, looked at Ward, and said, "I just no like being cooped up. Too much like prison."

"Not much we can do about that. Not 'til that storm dies down on Twelve Mile Summit so the freight sled can get through, anyway," Ward replied. "Besides, Burkall's on his way from Chicken. He should be here today or tomorrow, and I ain't leavin' 'til he gets here."

Charlie looked back at his coffee cup and snickered a little.

Ward felt anger flame up at the thought of someone laughing at him. With a leveled, measured tone, Ward asked, "What's so funny?"

Without looking up, Charlie said, "Chicken. Why you call it Chicken?"

Ward relaxed, realizing Charlie was not laughing at him, after all.

"The old-timers were going to call the town Ptarmigan, but nobody could spell it. So, they all agreed to call it Chicken."

Still inspecting his coffee mug, Charlie snorted and said, "Silly white mans."

The front door of the roadhouse swung inward, letting in a foggy rush of supercooled air and snowflakes that rushed along the floor and then vanished as it mingled with the stale, warmer inside air. The door slammed shut, revealing a large man with an ice-encrusted beard, fresh from the trail. Throwing back his fur-ruffed parka hood and removing his mittens, the stranger studied the patrons' faces. His eyes lingered briefly on Frank Ward and

Indian Charlie as he warmed the icicles in his beard with his hand. He pulled the ice free, then, grabbing the lapels of his parka, the stranger gave it a quick shake to rid it of snow before pulling it over his head.

"Speak of the devil," Ward said, half aloud as he watched the newcomer.

The stranger made his way to the barrel stove in the center of the room, stretched out his reddened, cold-stiffened fingers toward the heat, and bellowed, "COFFEE!"

Rubbing his hands together, he glanced around at the other patrons, who by now had turned their attention back to their own affairs.

Dressed in a red-and-white striped shirt with the sleeves rolled up, black trousers, and a white apron, the roadhouse owner brought him a steaming ceramic mug of coffee and said, "Two bits and free refills."

The stranger paid him, cradled the mug with both hands as if he was holding a baby bird, and then guzzled the hot, black liquid. Handing the mug back to the owner, the stranger simply stated, "Refill," then made his way toward Ward and Charlie. The stranger sat down next to Ward with his back to the wall and said, "It's been a while."

"Yes, it has...Indian Charlie, this here is Paul Burkall. Paul, this is Indian Charlie. Me and him was bunkmates at Stoney Mountain prison for a couple of years."

Ward watched as the two acknowledged each other with a quick nod of their heads, and sized each other up.

The owner returned with another mug of coffee for Burkall and a full pot to re-fill Ward and Charlie's mugs. Ward noticed him carefully looking at each of them as he poured. Two days earlier, Ward had caught the owner eyeing him and Indian Charlie. Ward had passed it off as idle curiosity of strangers new to the settlement. However, with the arrival of Burkall, the man's interest seemed to be renewed in all three of them. It vaguely concerned Ward, so he filed it away in the back of his mind to deal with later.

"Must be thirty below out there with the wind blowin'," Burkall stated, as the owner walked away. "But it's lettin' up some. I figure it'll blow itself out by mornin'."

"Hope so," Ward replied, as he watched the owner walk away. He took a sip of coffee, set it down, and continued. "The freighter sleds are ready to head out and we got passage on them. They figure four or five days to Fairbanks."

"You got this Laird fella located?" Burkall asked.

"Billy Smith's been keepin' tabs on him for me. Last I heard, Laird was runnin' mail for the railroad somewhere between Fairbanks and Seward."

Burkall took a sip of coffee, set it down, and slowly rolled the cup back and forth between the palms of his hands, then asked, "What's this Dalton Laird fella done that he needs killin' so bad?"

Ward noticed Charlie look at Burkall with wide eyes, then quickly back down at his mug. Ward involuntarily reached up and rubbed his notched left ear, remembering that day in the Amanita Saloon eight years before when Dalton took Ward's knife away from him, slammed him down on the table in front of the syndicate gang, and pinned his ear to the table.

To Ward's way of thinking, it was Dalton's fault Ward had spent eight years in prison. Then there was Corrine—he girl he loved. In his mind, the girl he could've had if it hadn't been for Dalton. He felt the old familiar flush rush over his face as anger once again almost overpowered him. He fought it down, swallowed his anger, and said, "I've got my reasons."

* * *

The next morning was clear and cold. The green, blue, and red ribbons of the northern lights weaved lazily across the star-studded black sky. Ward, Charlie, and Burkall ate a hasty breakfast alone under the watchful eye of the roadhouse owner, then donned their parkas. They headed to the three freight sleds with the horse teams already hitched and ready to go. Ward noticed a few other passengers making their way to the sleds, as well.

"Step lively, gentlemen. We've no time to waste," the wagon master called.

"Sir," Ward said, getting his attention. "I believe I left somethin' behind. I'll be back in two minutes."

The wagon master answered with a frown. "Make it quick."

Ward turned, told Charlie and Burkall to 'stay here,' then headed back to the roadhouse.

Ward stepped inside, looked around, and then quietly closed the door. No one was in the room but Ward could hear the owner rustling about in the kitchen. Ward pulled a knife from under his parka, turned the blade so it was pressed against his right forearm, and slipped it up his parka sleeve. Quickly crossing the room, Ward snuck through the kitchen door and caught the owner by surprise.

"What the—"

Ward took three long strides and grabbed the man's collar with his left hand. As Ward watched the man's eyes grow wide, he said, "Shh. You been eyeballin' me for the last few days. Why?"

"I...I just thought I knew you, is all."

"Yeah? From where?"

"The Amanita...in Fa-Fairbanks."

That's what I figured, Ward thought, as the familiar hot flush of anger flooded his veins. Only this time, he did not force it down.

"Sorry, but I just can't have word gettin' around too soon that I'm back in this country."

Ward extended his right arm to expose the blade, spun it around, and drove it deep into the man's heart.

Ward watched him gasp. A feeling of satisfaction cooled Ward's veins.

Pulling the knife free, Ward spun him around, grabbed him by the hair and slit his throat. Ward guided him to the floor to avoid the spewing blood.

A lifeless thing now twitched on the floor where the man once stood.

Reaching down, Ward wiped the blood from his knife on the man's apron, replaced it in his scabbard, and then slipped unseen out the back door.

He made his way to the freighters.

CHAPTER 2

"HAW!" DALTON LAIRD YELLED TO his lead dog. Annie dutifully swung left and the rest of the team of nine, quarter-wolf sled dogs pulled the sixteen-foot freight sled with its six hundred pounds of mail and freight up the bank of the Nenana River and onto the main street of Healy Fork. It had been a long haul. Driving through most of the night, Dalton was looking forward to a hot meal and some sleep.

Dalton stood on the brake board and plowed a furrow in the hard-packed snow of the street as they stopped in front of the combination post and telegraph office.

"Whoa, there puppies. Time to rest...we've earned it."

"MAIL'S IN!" someone yelled from inside.

Dalton stomped the snow hook into the street's packed-down snow and checked the dogs' feet, one-by-one, starting with Annie, the lead dog.

"Have a good trip, Mr. Laird? You're early," someone asked.

Dalton turned and glanced toward the voice. It was Ted, a young man of about twenty who had a child-like mind. Ted had just stepped out onto the boardwalk.

Dalton turned his attention back to his dogs and said, "Not too bad. There's a few open leads in the ice on the upper Nenana at Broad Pass, but the railroad sub-contractors have cleared and graded some of the right-of-way, which makes for a good wide trail. What time is it, anyway?"

"Just past eleven a.m. on the thirteenth of December. My birthday." Ted stepped down off the boardwalk. He untied the ropes that lashed the tarp over the sled load. "The sun's been up for about fifteen minutes now."

Dalton turned to Ted. "Your birthday, huh? Well, hope it's a good one. Goin' to spend it with your family?" Instantly, Dalton regretted asking the question. He'd forgotten Ted never knew his father and that his mother had left him behind here in Healy Fork last year as she was passing through. No one ever knew what became of her. "Sorry, Ted. I didn't mean to..."

"Aw, that's alright," Ted said as he frowned and looked down at the ground.

Dalton finished checking the dogs' pads then turned to help Ted with the ropes. As he did so, he glanced south, the direction from which he had just come, and noticed a rare phenomenon.

"Why looky there. I haven't seen one of those in a while," Dalton said. "Sun dogs."

Ted straightened up and his eyes followed Dalton's. Just above the horizon where the sun had risen, appeared three suns, side-by-side. As they watched, the two outside suns slowly faded away.

"Well, that was a nice birthday present. Kinda purty, wasn't it?" Ted asked, as he turned back to the tied down tarp.

"Yeah, it was," Dalton agreed.

"That railroad's gonna make a lot of changes in this territory..." Dalton glanced over at him as Ted spoke, taking his mind off the sun dogs. He noticed a slight smirk on Ted's face. "...might even put you mushers out o' business."

Dalton thought a bit, and then answered, "It could, but there's still all the villages in the bush that need supplies and mail in the winter."

He pulled the tarp off the load.

"That's true. But if that contraption I saw five years ago... what was it... back in 1913 in Fairbanks, ever catches on, that'll surely be the death knell for ya." Ted tossed a fifty-pound bag of mail onto the boardwalk.

Dalton's curiosity was aroused. "What contraption is that?" He grabbed a bag of mail.

"They called it an aeroplane. Some guy and his wife...um, the Martins, I believe their name was, rode in a machine about two hunnert feet up in the air over our heads. And fast, too. Someone said they was travelin' forty-five miles an hour. They wasn't suspended by no wires or nothin'. They just floated along in midair."

Dalton tossed the bag of mail onto the boardwalk beside the other bag, straightened up, looked at the youngster a minute, and then decided he was telling the truth.

"You don't say? I've heard of them aeroplanes." Then, he looked down at the ground as he continued, "Didn't know they brought one to Fairbanks, though. Ain't never seen one."

"You sure missed out on a grand spectacle. Yes, sir, that was a sight to behold."

Dalton thought a bit, shook his head, and spoke half aloud, "Even more change. My wife told me once 'it's called progress.' Oh, well..." Looking up at Ted, Dalton asked, "How much freight and mail ya got goin' out?"

"About three hunnert pounds."

"Well, I've still got about five hundred here. I'll unload the rest while you haul those two bags inside. Bring what ya got out and stack it with my freight. I'll go round up the other musher. You seen Frank Tondro around the camp?"

"Who?" Ted asked.

"Tondro... 'The Malamute Kid'."

"Oh...no. But if he's around, he's prolly over at the cookhouse spinnin' his yarns."

Dalton finished unloading the sled while Ted brought out the mail and freight and added it to the load destined for the Nenana railroad construction camp and Fairbanks beyond. Then, pulling the snow hook, Dalton gave the command "HIKE!"

Nine dogs with an empty sled, except for Dalton holding on for dear life, sped down the street to the small house he'd built not far from the construction camp headquarters. En route, Dalton noticed there weren't as many people in the community as there were earlier that summer.

He fed the dogs cooked rice and a dried salmon apiece, watered them, and then bedded them down on fresh dried grass—cut and stacked the summer before for that purpose. After cleaning up and changing clothes, he headed back to the post and telegraph office to see if there were any messages from Corrine. There weren't.

He wished Healy Fork had a telephone system like Nenana because he longed to hear Corrine's voice. He knew that wouldn't happen until the railroad tracks arrived in another year or two.

His stomach growled, reminding him he'd not eaten since the day before. He headed to the cookhouse—a long building used to feed the railroad construction crew. Food was always available.

As he walked through the door, Dalton noticed a few laborers and contract workers sitting together or by themselves, scattered around the dining area.

Three men sitting together at one of the tables turned in unison to look him over. By their dress, Dalton knew they were mushers or mail runners like himself. The Malamute Kid was walking back to that table with his trigger finger crooked through the handle of a cup of steaming coffee.

The Kid stopped, looked Dalton over, and said, "Hey, ya old Sourdough. Made it, I see. And early, too. How's the trail from Talkeetna?"

Dalton looked him over and smiled because The Kid never failed to amuse him.

The Kid was a show-off. He wore seal-fur pants and mukluks, and his fancy squirrel-skin parka with a wolverine ruff hung by the door. He was about forty-five years old, right at five feet tall and probably weighed a hundred pounds, soaking wet. Nevertheless, he was a heck of a dog driver. One of the best.

"Pretty good. A few open leads on the river, but the right-of-way, where it's cleared and graded, has a good bottom. You should make good time to Fairbanks. The mail's waitin' for ya at the post office, all stacked and ready to go," Dalton made his way to the coffee pot. "It looks to be about eight hundred pounds or so, of course..." Dalton paused and poured a cup of coffee, then turned to The Kid and said, "With your team, that shouldn't be any trouble. What are ya runnin' now, thirty-five dogs or so?"

Dalton watched the other men's faces and saw a few smirks and grins as they glanced at each other.

The Kid was known for driving thirty or more dogs at a time during the winter, with up to a hundred dogs in his kennel. He always took good care of them but finding enough food to keep them fed through the summer months was a chore.

"Thirty, actually," The Kid said. "I'm five short. Loaned 'em out to another driver the other day who had a heavy load of freight. A big ol' fat woman headin' to the states."

Dalton snickered to himself and turned back to the food table. Looking it over, he realized there was no hot food. Just sandwich makings. Mildly irritated, he piled his plate with cold roast beef and sourdough bread to build a sandwich.

"Ya know... if you was to get rid of them Indian dogs and get some wolf-dog cross-breeds like mine...," Dalton finished piling his plate with food and turned back to The Kid, "You wouldn't have so many to feed and they'd do twice the work."

The other men snickered.

Dalton sat down at the table while he watched The Kid's face turn red.

"Oh, don't even start, Dalton. I like my little Indian dogs. Besides, I wouldn't trust your wolf-dogs any further than I could throw 'em. I've seen too many of 'em turn on a man. You never know what they're thinking inside that wolf brain of theirs."

Dalton picked up his sandwich, looked at the other men, and said, "Well, I wouldn't worry about it none. You wouldn't even make an hors d'oeuvre for one of my dogs." He took a bite of his sandwich.

The other men laughed out loud.

The Kid stood up and said with consternation in his voice, "Go ahead and laugh. One of these days those dogs will eat ya. Mark my words. Besides, my dogs are way faster 'an yours!"

Dalton tried not to laugh with a mouth full of food but couldn't help himself. Finally, he swallowed and said with a smile, "Yes, you're right. Your dogs *are* faster than mine.

I agree. I'm sorry, I was only joshin' ya. Now sit back down."

The Kid looked around at the others and then plopped down on the bench.

"Kid, you're a good musher. One of the best. And I wouldn't want to hurt your feelin's for anythin' in the world," Dalton said as he stuck out his hand. "Friends?"

The Kid looked at him for a moment, smiled, took Dalton's hand, and said, "Friends."

"You gonna stay in Fairbanks for Christmas?" Dalton asked The Kid, changing the subject.

"Yep. You?"

"I wired Corrine a couple a days ago to meet me here. We're gonna spend some time alone in our cabin up the Stampede Trail on the Savage River and do some trappin'. Just her, my son Jackson, and me." Dalton's mind drifted for a couple of seconds as their images floated to the surface. "I sure miss 'em. I was kinda hopin' they would've gotten here by now." He raised his coffee cup for a sip.

Setting his cup down, he changed the subject again, "Hey, guess what I saw. A sun dog."

"This morning? You saw it this morning?" White Moose Ned asked.

"Yeah. About a half-hour ago."

"Well, you know what the ancient Greeks used to say about that, don'tcha?"

"No, I guess I don't," Dalton replied.

"They used to say sun dogs in the morning was a sure sign of an approaching storm. A bad omen."

"What about seein' 'em in the evenin'?"

White Moose scratched his whiskers. "Don't know. Ain't never heard about seeing 'em in the evening. Maybe 'clear as a bell and cold as...' aw, never mind."

"Yeah, that's what I thought. I never put much stock in superstition. So, what's new around here?" Dalton took another bite.

Laughing Ollie looked around at the others, then said, "Dalton, I gotta tell ya, there's a new guy hangin' around camp. He's been hittin' the bottle some and talkin' smack about somebody gettin' their comeuppance. He bandied about your name some, too. Been lookin' fer ya."

Dalton swallowed. "Really? What's his name?"

"Don't know his name. Says he's waitin' for some friends to show up. That's all I know."

Dalton looked over at The Kid.

Shrugging his shoulders, The Kid said, "I don't know anymore 'en he does, 'cept that he's been behavin' himself. Ain't broke no laws that I know of."

Dalton looked into the faces of each man, searching for more information. No one seemed to have anything else to add.

The Kid stood, drained the last of his coffee, and then exhaled with a satisfied sigh, belched, then said, "Well boys, wish me luck on the trail. I've got a lot of mail to haul and I best be gettin' to it."

The Kid walked to the door, took his parka off the coat peg and pulled it on.

"Careful crossin' the Tanana ice," Dalton warned. "I heard it's snowin' pretty good up north, and as warm as it is, there's probably overflow."

"Yeah, I figured as much," The Kid pulled his martin-fur hat out of his parka pocket. "And you watch yerself around that character. There's somethin' about him I don't like."

With that, The Kid put his martin hat on, opened the door and stepped out, shutting the door behind him.

Luck to ya on the trail, Kid, Dalton thought, as he took another bite of his sandwich. As he chewed, he wondered who the person they'd been talking about might be. *And why is he looking for me? I could use some sleep but that'll have to wait, I guess. I think I'll have a talk with the district engineer instead,* he decided. *See if he knows anything.*

Dalton finished eating, bid the other mushers 'farewell,' pulled on his parka, and headed for the engineer's office.

Stepping up on the porch, Dalton read the sign above the door:

FRANK H. BAILEY-DISTRICT ENGINEER

ALASKA ENGINEERING COMMISSION

Rapping on the door brought a response from within.

"Come in."

Pushing the door open, Dalton stepped in, moved to his left, and made eye contact with Frank Bailey.

Bailey stood at a file cabinet and appeared to be removing files and stuffing them into an attaché case.

"Well, hello, Dalton. How's the trail?"

Dalton smiled briefly and said, "Fine... fine," as he removed his parka and sat down in front of Bailey's desk.

"Just getting ready to close down the office for the winter. What can I do for ya?" Bailey sat down and leaned back in his chair.

"Well, sir, I understand there's been a man askin' around camp about me. Know anything about it?" Dalton asked.

Bailey looked at Dalton for a couple of seconds, shook his head and snorted lightly, then smiled as he looked away then back at Dalton.

"Yes, I do. One of my foremen told me about him."

Dalton waited, but Bailey offered no more information.

"Well, do you know his name and what he wants?"

"Calls himself William or Billy Smith. The foreman recalled seeing him around Fairbanks a few years back. He was sure this Mr. Smith was part of the Interior Syndicate. Say, didn't you have something to do with breaking up that gang?"

Dalton looked away to nothing in particular and searched the recesses of his mind, reliving the highlights of that period.

Yukon Jacks' ripped and bloody face appeared and faded as other memories surfaced and then faded. Memories of Ward with a knife, pinning his ear to a tabletop. Of Bandit his lead dog—strong, loyal and true until the end. Of Corrine, soft and warm by his side as the guns of Jon Batiste and the syndicate blazed away at their cabin. A black wolf. The northern lights.

It all came back with a rush and then faded away.

Looking back at Bailey, he said, "Yes... yes, I did. He did some time in the Fairbanks jail, got out, then left town. I haven't heard of him or the rest of the gang in years."

"Well, if this guy has some kind of vendetta in mind," Bailey leaned forward. "Keep it outside the camp. I don't have many laborers as it is because of the winter slow-down and the ones I got, I can't afford to lose from fear of getting killed, or whatever."

Dalton stood, looked down at Bailey, and noticed his eyes widen. "I'll do what I can, but I ain't makin' no promises. Can ya tell me where I can find him?"

Bailey looked Dalton up and down briefly, and then said, "I reckon you can find him at the roadhouse in Lignite—up the trail about four miles. Non-AEC personnel aren't allowed to stay in the work camp."

CHAPTER 3

CORRINE REMOVED HER BEAVER-FUR MITTEN, reached down to her six-year-old son, Jackson, and pulled the knitted scarf up to cover his small nose. Although the weather had warmed up some and it was snowing lightly, she knew the breeze caused by the moving, four horse-drawn, open-bob sled stage they were riding in could freeze exposed skin in a matter of moments.

The melodious jangling of the bells on the horse collars as they traveled the trail, plus the creaking of cold-stiffened wood joints and the squeaking of steel-clad runners on hard-packed snow, created a white noise that lulled one into slumber.

Sitting on the outside edge of the first bench seat on the stage, she faced rearward. The other two bench seats faced forward. Three people per bench. Luggage was stowed on the tailgate and under the bench seats.

Feeling a bit self conscious, Corrine replaced the mitten on her hand and scanned the faces of her fellow passengers. They were all dressed pretty much the same—in heavy fur coats and hats. Some had scarves to cover their ears, mouth, and nose. Each row of passengers shared a large fur blanket, provided by the stage line, to place across their laps and drape over their knees to the floor.

She decided most of the passengers seemed to be employees of the railroad headed to Nenana, the main construction camp for the northern end of the rail. Maybe one or two were going further, as she was, on to Healy Fork.

Her mind drifted then, as she thought about the railroad. She knew many people believed it would breathe new life into the dying mining town of Fairbanks. The yellow metal had dropped to ten percent of what the mines had been producing. People were leaving every day and many homes now stood vacant in a once-bustling city. One thing was certain, she decided, it would bring a change of some kind. Not only for the white man but for her mother's people, as well.

Dalton's on-call work in law enforcement didn't pay much. Most of the native children she taught were now out on the trap lines with their families. Unfortunately, the price of fur had dropped in the Seattle fur market, making it hard to make ends meet. The only real money to be made now seemed to be working for the Alaska Engineering Commission. Therefore, Dalton had taken a contract to run mail and freight between steel from Talkeetna to Healy. Last fall, together, they had built a home—close to Healy so they could be together more often.

Healy. She looked down then at Jackson and smiled, thinking of Healy, for Dalton was there now, waiting for her and their son. It had been over two months since she and Dalton had spent time together and the weight of anticipation had grown heavier and heavier.

Soon, she thought, *we'll be together. A family once again.*

The sleigh suddenly swayed a little as the front left runner bottomed out in a slight depression in the trail, jolting her back into the present. She quickly looked at Jackson to make sure he was okay. Seeing that he was, she again scanned the faces of the others. One gentleman in the middle seat of the next row facing her made eye contact and smiled.

"Everything okay, ma'am?"

"*Aaha,*'," she said, dropping her eyes from his. Sometimes, under stress, she slipped into her mother's Gwich'in Athabascan native tongue.

"Say, aren't you... Aren't you Dalton Laird's woman?"

Quickly looking back up at him and then away again, she said, "*Aaha*'...um, yes, I am."

"Thought so. Proud to make your acquaintance," he tipped his Bowler hat to her.

She glanced back at him, flashed a quick smile, and nodded to him as she turned her attention back to Jackson.

Seeing he rested comfortably, she glanced around and noticed that the snowflakes, falling sideways past the moving stage, had grown bigger and more abundant. *Looks like we are going to get a lot of snow,* she thought. Then, her mind drifted back to Dalton.

She'd been packed and ready when he sent the message to meet him in Healy, and she left immediately. She looked forward to spending time alone with him in their Savage River cabin on the Stampede Trail.

It was located in some of the most beautiful country she had ever seen. Close to Deenadheet, or Mount McKinley, as the white people were calling it. Game was abundant there. Wild berries grew in profusion in the valleys and the fur was prime and luxurious—a perfect place to raise a family.

She remembered when they were building their cabin how she'd gone exploring and found evidence that others, in times long past, had thought so, too. Depressions dug deep in the ground were evidence of living quarters, once covered with a wooden frame and sod.

She found stone implements like scrapers and projectile points and wondered what life was like for her mother's people in the old days.

Jackson stirred, and caught Corrine's attention. He shivered a bit, looked up at his mother, and said, "Cold."

Corrine removed her lap blanket, shook the accumulated snow from it, and helped little Jackson crawl up under her loose-fitting parka and onto to her lap. He snuggle close to her breast. With his head sticking out of her parka, just under her chin, she replaced the lap blanket.

"Just a little further, son, and we will stop in Nenana at the roadhouse. We can warm up there by the fire and then head on to Healy."

"Papa be there?"

"No, not in Nenana. He is in Healy. Papa will be in Healy."

Jackson didn't complain and seemed to accept his fate as he dozed with the swaying of the sleigh.

He has much of his father in him, she thought.

She smiled, thinking how nice it would be to take a break from this rough-riding sleigh with hot tea by the fire. She envisioned a fireplace with crackling flames.

In her vision, the flames grew and surrounded her and Jackson. Her smile left as apprehension and panic overtook her. She fought down the panic, and as she did so, the flames in her vision died down, as well.

What did that mean? she wondered. *Is Dalton alright?*

"Driver? How much longer before we reach Healy?" she asked.

Over his shoulder, the driver replied, "Ma'am, with all this snow coming down, we're gonna have to spend the night in Nenana and try to make Healy tomorrow."

CHAPTER 4

T ABOUT 1:00 P.M., DOC walked into the Healy Fork cookhouse and noticed the three mushers sitting at a table, drinking coffee. As he closed the door, they turned to look at him.

"Hey, Doc," Siwash Jimmy greeted.

"Gentlemen," Doc replied.

After hanging up his parka, and as the men continued their conversation, Doc walked over to the food table and poured himself a cup of coffee. As he poured, he overheard one of the men mention Dalton Laird's name in low tones.

"Dalton?" Doc asked, as he sat the coffee pot down. "Is he in?"

The men looked up at him.

"Yeah... You just missed him," replied Laughing Ollie.

Doc walked over to the table, sat down, took a sip of coffee, and then said, "I need to talk to him about something."

White Moose Ned looked at the others, then looked at Doc and said, "If what you want to talk to him about is that scoundrel lookin' fer him, we already told 'im."

Doc looked him in the eyes. "That's exactly what I want to talk to him about. I know who he is. Recognized him right off."

Doc looked down at his coffee, gave a little sigh, and then took a sip.

"Well?" Siwash Jimmy asked. "Who is he?"

Doc sat his coffee cup down, and said, "Billy Smith. He was a member of the Interior Syndicate. A peon, actually. Just a petty thief."

"How do you know him?"

Doc took another sip of coffee, set it down, and stared at his cup as he thought over his response.

"Well, I've known Dalton for years. I'm the one who took care of Yukon Jack and sewed up Bandit's knife wound in St. Joseph's Hospital. After Dalton broke up that gang, I followed the legal proceedings afterward. Billy got off with less than a year."

"So, you think, after all these years, this here Billy fella is lookin' for revenge?" asked White Moose.

Doc looked at him and said, "No...no Billy doesn't have the guts for it. But still, something about it bothers me."

Just then, Dalton walked through the cookhouse door.

"There he is," Doc said, loud enough for Dalton to hear. "We was just talking about ya."

Dalton turned his head and looked the group over. "Behind my back, I see," he said, as he took off his parka and tossed it on one of the tables.

"Oh, it's all good," Doc said.

Dalton walked to the table, sat down, and looked around at the men.

"So, what's up?"

"You remember Billy Smith?" Doc asked.

"Yeah, I just talked to Bailey about him. Guess he's hangin' out at the Lignite Roadhouse."

"Well, I was telling the boys about him and..."

Suddenly the door flew open and in rushed Ted from the post and telegraph office.

"Anyone seen Dalton?" he asked, breathlessly.

"Yeah, he's over here," said Laughing Ollie.

Doc watched with concern as Ted closed the door and hurried over to the table.

"Got an urgent telegram from Marshal Brenneman for ya," he said, as he handed the telegram to Dalton. After taking a couple of gasps to catch his breath he continued, "Ran all the way... from your place... looking for ya."

"You need to be careful about that," Doc warned. "You could frost your lungs."

"I know... but I figured this was important."

Turning to Dalton, Doc asked, "What's it say?"

"It says..." Dalton began slowly, "Frank Ward and someone by the name of Indian Charlie escaped Stoney Mountain Prison a few weeks ago in Canada. Witnesses claim to have seen two men fitting their descriptions crossing the border back into the territory. Also, information was received from Fort Yukon that the owner of the Tanana Roadhouse in Circle City had his throat slit a few days ago. Three newcomers to the area were seen in Circle about that time. Two of them fit Ward and Indian Charlie's descriptions. The third one, no one knows."

"Well, that cinches it," Doc said.

"Cinches what?" Dalton asked, looking up at Doc.

"It all adds up. Billy, a member of the old gang looking for ya and at the same time making comments about someone getting their just deserts. Ward's escape from prison, making his way back to the territory... it looks like they're putting the old gang back together and it's you they're coming after. I think you need to head for the hills. Lay low for a while 'til this blows over. You don't need this kind of trouble."

"Well, we certainly don't need this kind of trouble associated with the railroad," White Moose said. Doc looked at Ned as he raised his cup of coffee.

"We don't need problems like this anywhere," Siwash Jimmy interjected with anger in his voice. "We just gained territorial status four years ago, and Wickersham is pushin' for statehood in Congress. They already think we're a bunch of ignorant prospectors and trappers livin' like the old west days. Why, if this turns into a shoot-um-up, they'll get wind of it sure enough and—"

"I agree with Doc. Head down to Anchorage and let the US Marshal deal with it," interrupted Laughing Ollie.

Doc looked back at Dalton, who was staring at the telegram.

"No...I can't do that." Dalton said. "If what you say is true, I can't run. I gotta face 'em."

* * *

Dalton stepped off the porch of the cookhouse and headed toward his house. It'd been a good twenty-four hours since he had had any sleep. His brain was a little foggy as the events of the last two hours replayed in his mind.

He decided not to worry about Billy right then. He was more concerned about Corrine and Jackson.

Why weren't they here, yet? Was there trouble on the trail? Reports were that it was snowing pretty good up north.

Reaching his house, Dalton walked in and stoked the stove with a couple of lumps of coal. The bed looked inviting but he decided the place could do with some cleaning. Besides, if he went to sleep now, he might miss Corrine and Jackson's arrival.

Dalton washed dishes, swept, chopped wood, checked on the dogs, dusted...anything he could to kill time. Finally, he sat down and waited.

Dalton woke with a start at the realization of his sled dogs howling. Something had piqued their interest. Peering out the frosted windowpane, Dalton could just make out the form of the four-horse-drawn stage making its way down the main street. The faint jingle of sleigh bells brought a smile to his face.

At last, he thought. *My bride has returned.* Dalton picked up his parka and pulled it on as he stepped out the door.

"PAPA!" Jackson exclaimed, as Dalton walked up to the stage.

"Jackson, my son. Oh, how I've missed you. You been a good boy for Mama?" Dalton asked, as he picked Jackson up off the stage and held him in his arms.

"Yes."

"That's my boy."

Dalton reached into his pocket and handed Jackson a small carving, painted black.

Jackson took it and asked, "What is it?"

"It's a black wolf. I've been working on it just for you."

Jackson smiled and held it close. "Thank you, Papa."

Reaching up with his left hand, Dalton helped Corrine off the stage.

Holding Jackson in his right arm and caressing Corrine with his left, he said, "I've missed you."

Corrine smiled. "We've missed *you*."

Back at the house, Dalton helped Corrine unpack the two trunks she'd brought along, as he filled her in on the events that had transpired since his arrival four hours earlier.

"Right now, it's just speculation. I want to question Billy and try to find out what's going on," Dalton said, as he watched Jackson playing on the floor. "I think I'll head down to Lignite in the morning."

Dalton looked over at Corrine as she folded clothes and put them away in the dresser drawers. She was silent.

This isn't good, Dalton thought. *Obviously, something is bothering her.*

He hated to ask the question, but he needed to know her opinion. It was important to him.

"So...what are your thoughts?"

Silence.

"Well?" he prodded.

She threw the last article of clothing she was folding into the drawer and slammed it shut.

"You do not want to know what I am thinking," she quipped, as she turned away.

"Um...yes, I do. That's why I asked."

"Go do whatever you gotta do," she snapped over her shoulder as she folded more clothes.

"Honey, what's wrong?"

"Nothing!"

"Something's wrong."

"I am just tired. I am tired of the long trip. I am tired of the dark. I am tired of you chasing bad guys. I am tired of my father's influence over our lives even in death. I thought we were through with all that."

Then, turning back to him with tears in her eyes, she said, "I thought we were going to be a family again. Just you, me, and Jackson—all by ourselves. Every time something happens, it is you they call, and I do not know if you will come back alive or dead. If this turns out the way you think, why do you have to deal with it? Let someone else do it!"

Dalton fought down the anger welling up inside. Looking down at Jackson playing on the floor, he thought a bit, looked back at Corrine and said with a level, measured voice, "If you don't know, I can't explain it to you. I can't run."

"Maybe not. But I can. Do not expect Jackson and me to be here if it happens."

CHAPTER 5

THE NEXT MORNING WAS SOMEWHAT warmer as Dalton quietly made his way to the coal shed behind the house to refill the coal bucket for the cook stove. Corrine and Jackson still slept and he didn't want to disturb them. Looking up, he noticed clouds had moved in during the night, which obscured the stars and the waning gibbous moon.

Maybe there's something to the ancient Greeks' belief about sun dogs in the morning, he thought. *Looks like a storm's a brewin'.*

As he filled the coal bucket, he thought about what he could do.

If Doc was right, and, indeed, Dalton tended to believe Doc *was* right, *and if reports are correct, Ward has two men with him. And then there's Billy Smith, as well. Four-to-one are not very good odds.*

Dalton carried the bucket of coal into the house and contemplatively stoked the fire and poked at the embers to create a good draw.

Checking his pocket watch, it read 7:15 a.m.

The telegraph office should be open, he decided. *I'll wire Marshal Brenneman and explain the facts as I know them. Perhaps he could send Deputy Marshal Wiseman to help handle this.*

Dalton stepped out of the house and into the dark. The snow seemed to be falling a little heavier. He pulled his parka about himself as he headed for the lights of the post and telegraph office. In the distance, he heard the little generator that produced power for the building's electric lights.

Dalton became suddenly aware of the soft swish of runners on hard-packed snow behind him. Looking back, Dalton stopped and watched a lone musher come into town from the north. Dalton and the musher made eye contact and Dalton recognized him. It was Billy Smith. Dalton then watched Billy pull up in front of the cookhouse and go inside.

Dalton quickly sent the message to Marshal Brenneman and waited a few minutes for the reply. The marshal responded that he could not provide anyone, and that Dalton should consider himself deputized and investigate the situation himself.

Dalton suddenly felt all alone.

Well, if that's the lay of it, there's no time like the present to talk to Billy. At least he saved me a trip to Lignite, he decided. Dalton took his Copenhagen from his pocket, took a dip, shoved the can back into his pocket and headed for the cookhouse.

Stepping into the cookhouse, Dalton closed the door and moved to the side. Quickly scanning the interior, he observed the usual crowd and Doc sitting at their table in front of him. In the far left corner, with his back to the wall, sat Billy.

Dalton noticed the men at the center table glance up at him and then back at their respective coffee cups. Doc looked at Billy then back at Dalton and gave a slight nod of his head toward Billy. Billy watched Dalton with a slight smirk on his face.

Billy Smith was somewhat short, a little on the heavy side, about five-foot-six, Dalton figured. He was dressed in gray wool bib coveralls that covered a red wool shirt. Remnants of frost from his frozen breath (from being on the trail in sub-freezing weather) glistened on his full beard and dripped down the front of his bibs. A tanned caribou-hide parka with the hair left on, lay on the table next to him.

Dalton hung his parka on the coat peg and walked to the opposite side of Billy's table and stood facing him. With Billy's back to the wall, this effectively blocked any escape attempt Billy might make. Dalton noticed Billy glance to his left and right and then his shoulders sag, evidently realizing the mistake he had made.

"Hear ya been lookin' for me," Dalton said matter-of-factly.

Billy spoke with a high pitched, nasally voice. "Maybe."

"No *maybe* about it," Dalton replied with an edge to his voice. "Either ya have or haven't. Which is it?"

Billy's eyes grew wide and he leaned back a little as he said, "Yeah, I been lookin' fer ya." And then a sort of smug look came across his face. He seemed to relax a little as he continued. "Got a message fer ya from Frank Ward. He's comin' after ya. He'll be here in a day or so."

"What does he want with me?"

"Ha! As if ya didn't know, mister smartypants. Ya know durn well whatcha did. Ya busted up the syndicate and got 'im sent to prison with them Mounties, is whatcha did. Worse 'en that, you stole his wuman."

At first, Dalton was shocked and then anger grew inside from a simmer to a boil.

Through clenched teeth, he said, "I didn't steal anyone's woman. Leave my wife out of this."

"Don't deny it. Ya know he was sweet on 'er. Ya think yer all high and mighty but he's got friends and we's comin' fer ya. Now, if you'll excuse me, I've got things to do."

Dalton looked him over a few seconds and then, slightly nodding his head, he said, "Tell him I'll be waitin'."

Billy rose and slowly sidestepped from behind the table as Dalton backed away to give him room to leave.

"I surely will, yes-sir-ree," Billy said as he picked up his parka and took a couple of steps toward the door. Then, over his shoulder, he said, "And it's too bad fer ya yer squaw's goin' ter be a wider soon. She'd make a right nice little addition to the gang."

Dalton clenched his jaw and took a step toward Billy. Billy scurried toward the door. Dalton stopped himself and let Billy go.

After Billy left the cookhouse, Dalton thought about the situation as his anger died down. He had not put a lot of stock in believing Doc's assumption that trouble was brewing, but Billy had pretty much proven Doc's theory correct.

Four men. Ward always was one to hide behind others, he thought. Back when Ward was a part of the syndicate, he always seemed to be on the outskirts and never directly in the line of fire.

A thought suddenly occurred to him. *Maybe I can whittle the odds down a little. I could arrest Billy for conspiracy to commit murder or something. After all, that's what he had just admitted to. Course, it might not stand up in court, but at least Billy will be out of the way.*

Dalton turned, walked back to the mushers and Doc sitting at the table, and said, "Well, looks like your suspicions were true."

Doc sighed and said, "Yeah, we heard. Now whatcha gonna do?"

As Dalton sat down, Laughing Ollie said, "I still say you should leave. Go to Anchorage until this thing blows over."

"I can't," Dalton said with a bit of irritation in his voice. "Ward ain't gonna let it '*blow over*,' as you say. Besides, this is my fight. It's got to end here."

Dalton took a deep breath, then exhaled. He said in a softened voice as he looked at each musher, "I would, however, appreciate all the help I can get."

Dalton watched as each quickly glanced at the other, then down at the table or their coffee cups.

"Yeah. That's what I thought," Dalton said as he stood up.

"Where're you headed?" Doc asked.

"I'm goin' to chase Billy down, arrest him and bring him back here. Keep him under lock-and-key. That should even the odds somewhat."

"Where ya gonna keep him?" Siwash Jimmy asked. "We ain't got a jail!"

Dalton picked up his parka, turned to the mushers and said, "I don't know. Maybe in the cellar at the boarding house. I'll figure something out."

Dalton pulled the parka on, jammed his fur hat on his head, and slammed the door as he left.

CHAPTER 6

IT WAS SNOWING HARDER AS Dalton walked through the front door of his house at 8:00 a.m. and found Corrine making breakfast. After shaking the snow from his parka, he hung it on a wall peg. He sat down at the table and watched her. She did not speak.

"Just had a run-in with Billy a few minutes ago," he ventured.

Still she held her tongue, so he continued.

"He confirmed that Ward and two others are on their way here. They should be here in a day or two, accordin' to Billy. I've decided I'm going after Billy and bring him back. Keep him under lock-and-key until this is over. At least there'll be one less to worry about."

"Can the marshal send someone to help?" she asked, as she continued making breakfast.

"No. I already asked. He told me to consider myself deputized and to take care of it."

Corrine did not respond.

Dalton clenched his teeth, rose from the table, and made his way to the bedroom. There, he watched Jackson, still clutching the wolf carving in his little hand and sleeping soundly in their bed. He leaned over and reached down to pull the blanket up to tuck around his son.

As he did so, Jackson woke, looked up, and asked, "Papa?"

"Yes, son. I'm here."

Jackson smiled.

Dalton smiled back at his son and said, "I have to go out for a little while. But I'll be back. Be good for Mama, alright?"

Jackson closed his eyes and nodded his head.

Dalton rose, opened a drawer of the dresser table, and removed his shoulder holster containing his Colt 1911 semi-automatic .45 and an extra magazine. After putting the holster on and adjusting the fit, he reached into the drawer and removed his US Marshal's badge. This, he pinned onto his shirt on his chest.

He saw his possibles bag hanging on the wall with extra socks, matches, mukluks, and other handy items one might need. He thought about bringing it. After second thought, he decided against it. After all, he reasoned he wouldn't be gone that long.

Back in the front room, he took his parka from the coat peg and put it on.

Then, to Corrine, he said, "I shouldn't be too long. He's stayin' at the roadhouse in Lignite, so I should be back by noon at the latest."

Corrine looked sideways at him, as she stirred something in a pot on the stove. She laid the spoon down and tossed him a brown paper bag.

"There's some sourdough biscuits and bacon. You will need food in your belly before you come back."

Dalton caught the package and placed it in his parka pocket.

"Thanks," he said. To test the waters and dispel tension, he added, "I love you."

She smiled, then. "I love you, too. Go do what you gotta do."

Dalton smiled back at her and thought, *Maybe she's coming around.* He turned and walked out the door.

* * *

The wind had picked up some and blew curly-cues of snow from the eve of the roof, swirling it across the hard-packed street.

Dalton stood on the brake board of his sled, pulled the snow hook, and stowed it away in the holster made for it which hung from the cross-brace of the handle bow. The wolf-dogs seemed eager to run and impatiently jumped up-and-down in their harnesses.

Annie dutifully kept the tugline taut and watched her master. Dalton smiled.

Dalton had not had much of a reason to smile lately, but the thought of an open four-mile trail to Lignite and the enthusiasm of the dogs tore down the wall of loneliness he was beginning to feel.

"At least I can count on you, Annie. HIKE!"

The wolf-dogs lunged into their harnesses and headed north into the dark, snowy night. Dalton kept just enough pressure on the brake to keep the bouncing sled and the dogs lined up, which produced a rooster tail of ice crystals as the brake plowed a furrow through the hard-packed snow.

After the dogs settled down and pulled in unison, Dalton released the brake completely. He fully trusted Annie to find the wind-drifted trail on her own because his eyes had not completely adjusted to night vision. Soon, however, he could sharply discern between the black silhouettes of trees and lighter blue-grays of snow.

Reaching into his pocket, he pulled his watch and a match out, hunched over the handle bow to block most of the wind, and struck the match. The quick flash of light illuminated the watch face. It read twenty minutes after eight.

Almost three hours 'til sunup, he thought, as he replaced the watch. *Billy's probably already in Lignite. A half-hour to get there, a half-hour to arrest him and get him loaded on the sled. A half-hour back to Healy...heck, I may be back before sunup.*

Twenty minutes later, Dalton pulled up in front of the Lignite Roadhouse, tied the sled to a post, and went inside. Closing the door and stepping to the side, Dalton quickly scanned the interior looking for Billy. Instead, he saw the owner, Colvin—a big Scotsman—sitting in a rocking chair by the wood stove, wearing glasses and mending a mukluk with needle and thread.

"Sit yourself down there, Laddie, and warm up a bit," he said to Dalton, as he indicated a chair by the wood stove.

"Thanks, but I'll stand." Dalton stepped to the stove and pulled off his mittens. Holding his extended hands toward the stove to warm them, he continued. "Lookin' for a fella by the name of Billy Smith. I was told he was stayin' here."

Dalton watched Colvin raise his bushy eyebrows and peer at him over the top of his glasses, then back at his sewing. "Aye, that he was."

"Was?"

"Aye. He is no longer here."

"Can you tell me where he went?"

Colvin laid the mukluk in his lap, removed his glasses, leaned back in his rocking chair, and said, "North is all I know. Either Nenana or Fairbanks. I told the laddie he was a fool to travel in this weather, but he was in an all-fired hurry to leave. Now I see why."

"How long ago?" Dalton asked as he replaced his mittens.

Colvin shrugged his shoulders. "Half hour, forty-five minutes?"

*   *   *

About eleven miles north of Lignite, the AEC right-of-way crossed to the east side of the Nenana River at Ferry work camp. Ferry, a smaller camp than Healy Fork, had already closed down for the winter and the construction crew relocated to Fairbanks to lay steel south. Now, abandoned canvas-walled tents, supported by spruce log structures with wood plank floors, faced the cleared right-of-way, waiting for the return of spring and the laborers.

Dalton braked his wolf-dogs to a halt in front of the tents and stomped the snow hook into the packed snow of the trail. Turning his head away from the wind and blowing snow, he pulled off his right mitten, reached up to his eyelashes, and, with his thumb and forefinger, melted the miniature icicles that encrusted them. Now that he could see better in the dim light, he quickly wiped the moisture off his fingers onto his parka, replaced the mitten, and stepped toward the nearest tent. As he did so, he noticed the tent flaps had been cut. They fluttered with the wind gusts. Looking down the row of tents, he could see the others had been cut open, as well.

Upon entering, he saw the mattresses that had once been neatly rolled up and placed at the head of each bunk were unrolled and strewn about the interior. Checking inside the other tents, he found the same. Barely visible tracks in the drifted snow revealed someone had been here recently, evidently looking for something. Dalton surmised that it was more than likely Billy Smith, looking for anything of value he could steal. Dalton smiled to himself as he realized Billy's larcenist nature might work to Dalton's advantage. All the time spent ransacking the tents allowed that much more time for Dalton to catch up to him.

Suddenly, Dalton's smile disappeared as he watched the wall of the tent heave in and out with the gusting wind. Twelve miles ahead, the trail breaks out of the foothills of the Alaska Range and onto muskeg flats that run a good twenty-five miles north to Nenana. Out there, there was nothing to stop or slow the wind and snow. The wind whipped ice crystals that could sandpaper your skin off in a matter of moments—wind chills a hundred below or more. With visibility less than five feet, he knew Annie could find the trail alright but he didn't relish the idea.

If I can catch him within the next twelve miles, I won't have to worry about that, he thought. *And if I can't? Well, he's signing his own death warrant. He's a fool to think he can make it across the flats.*

Dalton shivered as he turned to leave the tent. The intense cold had penetrated his parka and reached his sweaty undergarments. He knew he should probably stay right where he was—build a fire in the little Yukon stove and dry out. But duty called and the thought of Billy Smith getting away rankled him.

Pulling the snow hook, Dalton gave the command and the wolf-dogs responded with eagerness. Twenty minutes later, the brightening southern horizon behind him provided enough light to see well. In some of the more protected places from the wind, snow-filled parallel depressions on the trail revealed Billy Smith's passage. From the way the depressions were filling in with the blowing snow, Dalton surmised Billy was maybe thirty minutes or less ahead.

Dalton's toes were cold, and his feet were getting chilled. He held onto the handle bow of the sled and ran along between the runners to warm up. He knew his socks and the inside of his mukluks were damp from sweat. He wished now that he'd brought his possibles bag to change them. If he did not catch Billy soon, he'd have to stop and try to build a fire in this wind to dry them out.

Just before the flats, the right-of-way made a swing to the right, away from the Nenana River and stayed close under the last foothills of the Alaska Range. It was wooded with white spruce, birch, and aspen and provided some shelter from the wind.

Dalton stood on the brake and gave the command, "Whoa!"

Standing there on the runners, Dalton surveyed his surroundings. The relentless wind roared through the treetops and drifted snow over anything in its path. Out on the flats, the only thing that could be seen was a wall of white. He had not seen any sign of Billy leaving the trail. Of course, if Billy *had* left the trail, any sign would've quickly disappeared. If Billy was out there, he was on his own.

Dalton shivered as the cold crept into his garments and nipped at him. His feet and hands had been cold ever since leaving Ferry, despite the intermittent jogging behind the sled to increase blood flow to his extremities.

Better throw up a shelter and build a fire, he thought. *Try to dry out and warm up some. Maybe this wind'll die down.*

With cold-stiffened fingers, Dalton turned his wolf-dogs loose. Under a brush pile left by the right-of-way clearing crew, he was able to clear out a small space, somewhat protected from the wind.

With his back to the opening, Dalton faced the brush pile and gathered small, dry twigs. Taking off his mittens, he shoved his bare hands up under his parka and under his arms for a few moments to warm his stiff fingers.

The wolf-dogs curled up in the snow, covered their noses with their tails, and let the snow drift over them, creating a cozy insulated bed out of the wind, as their ancestors had done for millennia.

Dalton removed his hands from his armpits and quickly dug through his parka pocket for a match. With a shivering hand, he struck it and cupped it with the other hand. The sudden warmth on his palms felt good. As he reached toward the little pile of tinder, a sudden swirl of air snuffed out the flame.

Dalton's fingers grew colder and he began to lose feeling in them. He cupped his hands, then blew into them to warm them with his breath. Another match. Another fumbling attempt. This time, however, the tinder ignited and grew.

Dalton quickly added more tinder and soon had a good fire going. Extending his hands toward the flames, he enjoyed the warmth of it and the tingling in his hands, as his deadened nerve-endings began to wake up.

Lightning flashed suddenly and thunder reverberated and his head exploded in pain.

Dalton turned, and lightning flashed again as he sunk into the velvety blackness of unconsciousness.

CHAPTER 7

DALTON LAIRD FELT HIS BODY move. Then, he felt it again.

Opening his eyes, the brightness made him blink. Snow fell into his eyes. Dalton tried to sit up and wipe it away. An excruciating pain in his head made him groan and sway. Annie whined and nudged his body again as nausea overtook him. He pushed her away, rolled over, and threw up. There was nothing in his stomach but bile and stomach acids. The taste of the nastiness made him retch again. The dry heaves continued for a few seconds until finally, by sheer will power he made them stop.

He shivered as he reached out to grab some snow to clean his mouth. While rubbing his mouth, he realized he could not feel his face with his hand. His cheeks and nose didn't seem to have any feeling either.

He looked at his hand. It was like a cold, gray dead thing at the end of his arm. Rolling onto his back, he looked at his other hand

and then clapped them together. There was no feeling, no sensation. He tried to wiggle his toes. They, too, had no feeling.

Panic overtook him as he realized he was slowly freezing to death. Fighting down the panic, he assessed his predicament. How had he gotten into this situation? Why did his head hurt so much? Fire! That was the main thing. He needed fire!

He again tried to sit up and this time was successful. Fighting through the throbbing head pain, he forced himself to concentrate on the task at hand—plan out every detail with no wasted movement.

Looking around, he saw burnt sticks and ashes, and then realized he *had* built a fire earlier, and then something had happened. But what? *No matter,* he decided. *The fire's the thing. Build that fire!*

With trembling, cold-stiffened hands, he gathered more twigs and strips of birch bark by grasping them between both hands, pressed together in a prayer position. *Now, how am I going to get the matches out of my parka pocket?* Building the first fire, he'd had some control of his fingers. But now they were useless pieces of clay. Panic rose again. Dalton mentally fought it down.

Think! he told himself.

Suddenly, an idea. The butt-end of a small tree that had been cut and stacked in the brush pile, jutted out at just the right height so that Dalton could stand and hook the hem of his parka on it. As he knelt, the tree raised the hem of his parka, waist-high. This, in turn, gave him access to his sheath knife. With both hands in the praying position, he extracted the knife. All he had to do was cut his pocket open so the matches could fall out.

With the blade pointing downward and grasped between his two numb palms, Dalton stuck the blade into his pocket and sawed it up and down. The blade made two good cuts before he lost his grip. His hand slipped, flipping the blade out of his pocket. The knife made a somersault and landed point-first in the snow. Grasping the knife again, Dalton made another attempt, this time cutting the pocket to the bottom. Using his knife, he was able to scrape out the matches onto the powder dry snow. Only three appeared.

Laying his knife by the tinder bundle along with the three remaining matches, Dalton's shaky middle fingers reached toward a match and he gingerly picked it up. It slipped between his deadened fingers and fell back into the snow. On his second attempt he was successful. Striking it on the knife handle, the match sputtered to life as it flipped out of his grasp, only to sizzle and die in the snow. Panic again reared its ugly head, and again, he successfully fought it down.

Again, another try. Dalton struck the match once...twice. It would not light.

Last match. Dalton uttered a prayer, then struck the match on his knife handle. It caught. Carefully, Dalton moved it toward the pile of tender and, with trembling hands, held it under a piece of birch bark. The bark caught fire easily and grew, igniting the small dead spruce twigs and Old Man's Beard moss.

Ever so gently, Dalton placed more and more fuel on the fire as needed. The wind had died down. Things looked up and he smiled. Holding his hands to the flame, they tingled and ached as they thawed.

Only now did he allow himself to think about other things. He had spent this whole time facing and concentrating on the hollow in the brush pile and the little fire. Now he turned, pulled the side of his parka hood back, and looked around. Turning his head caused it to throb as he surveyed his surroundings. Annie and the other wolf-dogs sat in a half-circle behind him. Dalton turned back toward the fire and tested his hands. His fingers could move some, but not much. He placed more wood on the fire. Then he pulled more and more brush out of the pile and let it ignite. Soon, the whole brush pile would be engulfed.

Reaching up, Dalton attempted to pull his parka hood off but found that it was stuck to his hair and caused his head to hurt even more. Dalton reached up inside the hood and felt around. When he pulled his hand out, he saw that it was covered in blood.

His mind cleared some and he was able to put the pieces of the puzzle together. Dalton surmised that Billy had decided not to take a chance crossing the flats in the blizzard. Instead, he'd hunkered down to wait it out. When Dalton stopped to build a fire to warm up, Billy was close enough to see him. As Dalton worked the fire, and under the cover of the blowing snow so that neither Dalton nor the dogs could hear him, Billy made his move. He snuck up on Dalton with a club.

Dalton determined he'd been unconscious for only an hour or so. Evidently, Billy did not swing hard enough. That, along with the padding of Dalton's parka hood had saved Dalton's head, giving him a slight concussion instead of killing him. On the other hand, maybe that was Billy's only intention. Maybe he just wanted enough time to get away. If Billy had killed him, Dalton figured, that would've robbed Frank Ward of the satisfaction.

The brush pile was burning good and throwing a lot of heat. Dalton gingerly pulled his parka hood loose from his blood-matted hair, and then removed his parka, laid it on the snow, and sat on it. After warming his hands even more, he pulled his mukluks and socks off. He hung them on limbs by the fire to dry out, along with his mittens. His feet, he kept extended toward the fire. The tips of his toes were solid. He realized he might lose a toe or two. Soon, feeling returned to his feet as thousands of little pinpricks, and then an excruciating ache. Nevertheless, he knew he must endure the pain. He ate the sourdoughs and bacon as he concentrated on watching the steam rise from his socks and mittens and mukluks, and float away in the frigid, subarctic air.

An hour later, Dalton was thoroughly warmed. His socks and mittens were dry and warm, as well. His fingers ached as he gingerly pulled the socks over his throbbing toes. Pulling on the warm, dry mukluks locked warmth against his skin.

Hobbling around on painful feet, Dalton found Billy's camp. Traces of his sled trail in the drifted snow showed he'd headed out onto the flats. With the calm weather, he figured Billy was probably almost to Nenana by now. No use chasing him down. Besides, Dalton needed medical attention and the best place for that was back home.

Dalton painfully harnessed the wolf-dogs and pointed them toward Healy Fork. At nearly 2:45 p.m., with sundown about forty-five minutes away, Dalton pulled the snow hook and gave the command "HIKE!"

CHAPTER 8

FRANK WARD AND HIS MEN got off the freight wagons in Chatanika gold camp and quickly hopped the narrow gauge train to the construction camp of Happy, just north of Fairbanks. Ward did not want to go on into Fairbanks and risk being recognized. He reasoned the AEC construction camp was populated mostly by stateside workers, so there would be less chance of being recognized. There, they waited for a southbound stage to Nenana.

What had originated as a small community of Athabascan people at the mouth of the Nenana River as it empties into the Tanana, the village had turned into the headquarters of the AEC for the northern half of the railroad. Sternwheelers that had at one time supplied freight up the Tanana to Fairbanks since 1901, and now Nenana, sat in dry-dock or frozen fast in the Tanana ice. Docks lined the waterfront and new buildings populated once quiet wilderness lowland. A hospital, AEC office buildings, a power plant, and mercantile shops sprang up seemingly overnight. Residential lots had been laid out and were sold to the highest bidder. Water lines were buried in the muddy streets while power and phone lines were strung in the air.

Ward stepped off the stage and slowly looked around. A smile crossed his face. A lot had changed in the last eight years, he mused, and if a man had a mind to, he could make a killing here.

Then the smile disappeared as the thought of Dalton Laird crossed his mind.

Speakin' of killin', I've got other things to do, he thought.

* * *

Frank Ward sat at the table in the corner of the dining and bar area of the Nenana Roadhouse, killing time with Paul Burkall over a game of five-card stud. As was his habit, Ward glanced around the room.

The same three customers had been there for a while. Two trappers sat together at a table discussing the price of furs, and another man wearing a Bowler hat sat reading a newspaper nearby.

Movement in the corner of his eye caught Ward's attention and he looked back to the table. Burkall had laid down his hand. Ward held his breath as he looked at it. Aces and eights. Then, he smiled.

"What's the matter? Can you beat it?" Burkall asked.

Ward studied his cards and said, "No. No, I can't beat it. I only have two of a kind."

Ward laid his cards on the table. Two fours. Then, realizing Burkall must have seen the look on his face, explained.

"It's your hand. Aces and eights in spades and clubs is a dead man's hand. But you have an ace and an eight in hearts, so maybe that don't count."

Burkall frowned and reached for the cards. It was his turn to shuffle.

"Superstition. I believe a man makes his own luck."

The door opened. Indian Charlie walked in. Looking around, he made eye contact with Ward and Burkall. Charlie took off his mittens then removed his parka and hung it on the log wall's coat peg, and made his way to their table. Ward could tell something was on his mind.

"Musher from south just now. Over at dog barn."

"Mail carrier?" Ward asked.

"No. Sled empty. Man drive dogs hard with whip."

Burkall looked up at Ward. "Think it's your buddy, Smith?"

Ward thought a bit. "Maybe. Find out. If it is, bring 'im here."

Burkall stood and headed for the door as Ward absentmindedly watched him leave. His mind was on other things.

Chances are, it isn't Billy, he thought. *But if it is, and he has news of Dalton's whereabouts, then things just got more interestin'.*

Charlie helped himself to the coffee on the wood stove and made his way back to Ward's table, and sat down. Ward dealt a hand of solitaire.

A few minutes later, the door opened. Ward looked up and watched Billy Smith enter with Burkall close behind him. After hanging their parkas on the pegs, Burkall pointed Smith in the right direction. Smith tucked his thumbs under his coverall straps and strode to Ward's table. Burkall stood behind him.

At the table, Smith leaned forward and stuck out his hand.

"It's been a long time, Boss."

"Indeed." Ward made no effort to take his hand.

Smith straightened up, glanced at his hand, wiped it on the front of his coveralls, and stuck his thumb back under the strap.

Ward glanced around the room and made eye contact with the man in the Bowler hat. The man quickly looked back at his newspaper, then turned the page as if continuing to read. Ward felt the heat of his anger grow.

"Let's take this somewhere else," Ward said in a lowered tone. "Too many eyes and ears in here. Burkall, you and Billy head back out to the dog livery. Me and Charlie will be along shortly."

Ward paid no attention to their leaving. Instead, with his head lowered as if looking at his solitaire hand, and with his eyes just under the brim of his hat, he watched the man in the Bowler hat.

The man showed no interest in their leaving, apparently engrossed in whatever he was reading. A couple of minutes later, Bowler hat man folded his newspaper, stood, and headed upstairs. He never once glanced in Ward's direction.

Somewhat at ease, Ward turned to Indian Charlie and said, "Let's go."

Entering the dog livery, Ward found Burkall and Billy feeding Billy's dogs.

"So. Give me some good news, Billy. Tell me ya know where Dalton is."

Smith handed a dried salmon to one of the dogs, wiped his greasy hand on the front of his bibs, cleared his throat and said, "The last

I saw of 'im, he was out cold in the blizzard about twenty-five miles south of here."

Ward felt new rage seething just below the surface. He fought to keep it down. "What do you mean, 'out cold'?"

"Snuck up on 'im in the blizzard an' thumped 'im a good'un upside the head, is what I done."

"Why did you sneak up on him? What was he doin' out in that kind of weather?"

Billy glanced at the others and said, "I figure he was trailin' me."

"Now just why would he be followin' you? What'd you say to him?"

Billy took a small step back. "He must'a found out I was lookin' fer 'im. Got me cornered in the cookhouse is what he done. And made me tell 'im we was comin' fer 'im."

Ward watched Billy's eyes dart from one man to the next and take another step back. The anger that seethed just under Ward's surface grew to a boil.

"He *made* you say that, huh? The only thing I told you to do was locate him. Now the element of surprise is gone. He'll be waitin'! You sure you knocked him out? He ain't dead? 'Cause if he's dead, I will gut you like a fish. He's mine! You understand?"

"I unnerstand. And I'm purty sure he ain't dead. He's a tough old codger. I'm willin' to bet he's back in Healy Fork with his wife and kid."

Ward was taken aback a little by that news. He stared at Billy for a full minute as he felt his anger subside to a simmer. "How do you know his wife and ked are there?"

"They was on the stage that came through Lignite yesterday where I was stayin'. All I had to do was ask around to figure out who they were."

"You right-handed or left?" Ward asked Billy.

Billy looked down at his hands then back up at Ward. "Right. Why?"

"'Cause I wanna make sure you can still use your gun when the time comes." Ward glanced at Charlie and Burkall then nodded toward Billy.

The two men stepped toward Billy and each grabbed an arm—Burkall on the left and Charlie on the right.

"Put his left little pinkie on that stump there," Ward ordered, as he nodded to a short section of spruce wood standing on end.

Burkall and Indian Charlie wrestled Billy to the stump and forced him to kneel before it. Burkall forced Billy's left hand on the stump. Billy protested loudly. Charlie stood behind Billy, holding his right arm behind his back. Charlie covered Billy's mouth with his other hand.

Ward drew his knife and stepped forward. With a quick chop, the first knuckle of Billy's little finger flipped through the air, followed by a spray of blood and a muffled scream. It landed in the straw on the floor. A hungry Malamute strained at the end of its chain, reached out with its paw, and raked the finger close enough to gobble it down. Billy's scream through Charlie's hand barely made it across the livery.

Leaning close, Ward said, "I was gonna kill ya. But you brought me some good news, and an extra gun may come in handy later. Next time, do what I tell ya and nothin' else. Understand?"

Billy's wide eyes stared into Ward's. He aggressively nodded his head.

* * *

Back inside the roadhouse, Ward sat alone at the table and cut the deck. The queen of hearts appeared. Ward sighed.

"So, Corrine's there too. And she has a child."

Then an evil smile crossed his face.

CHAPTER 9

DALTON LAIRD LAY IN THE Alaska Engineering Commission hospital bed in Healy Fork. He hadn't got much sleep during the night because of the pain. Doc wouldn't let him go home. He had said he wanted to keep him overnight for observation because of the concussion. That morning depression set in—and anger too. Anger at himself because he hadn't been as prepared as he should've been—chasing Billy Smith through the blizzard the day before. He knew better. He'd made assumptions.

He learned a long time ago in his lawman years not to assume anything. *What was that old axiom? Aw yes... A.S.S.U.M.E. makes an ass of you and me.*

It can also kill you as it almost did him. He knew that. He just hadn't taken the time to think it through.

Frank Bailey, the AEC district engineer had made it plain he didn't want any trouble in camp. His words carried weight, answering directly to Thomas Riggs Jr, the co-commissioner of the northern, or Fairbanks division of this federal railroad project. By his attitude, Dalton knew he would get no help from the AEC. There had been talk and speculation of Pinkerton railroad police working undercover, investigating possible sabotage and theft from the federal government, but no one knew for sure.

The handful of deputy US Marshals in the third judicial district—an area roughly the size of the western continental United States—were on patrol, investigating murders, claim jumpers, bootleggers or whatever. He would find no help there.

Even Corrine had made a veiled threat to leave him. Once again, he suddenly felt so very alone.

All right, if that's the way of it, so be it. But I'm not runnin'. I refuse to back down to that two-bit chump. If he wants a fight to settle it once and for all, I'll sure 'nuff give it to him. Dalton took a deep breath, slowly exhaled and said aloud, "By myself, if I have to."

Dalton examined his bandaged and blistered hands. He could feel his bandaged feet under the thin hospital blanket. The tip of one big toe had turned black and the doc said he had removed it at the first knuckle. It throbbed, making Dalton acutely aware of its condition.

Dalton clenched his jaws. "And now, I'm a cripple."

"How's it going this morning, you old bush rat?"

Dalton turned his head toward the voice and watched as Doc and his nurse walked into the room.

"Suppose you tell me," Dalton answered.

A brief smile flashed across Doc's face as he approached Dalton's bedside.

"Well, let's take a look."

Doc folded back the bed sheet and blanket, unwrapped the bandaged foot with the amputated toe tip, and examined his handiwork.

"When can I get out of here? I don't like bein' all cooped up like this."

Doc glanced up at Dalton and then back at the toe. "Pretty soon. I'll have to think on it." Then, looking at his nurse he said, "Dorothy, bring me some picric acid, please. Oh, and some fresh bandages, also. Thanks, dear."

Dalton watched as Dorothy turned to leave, then turned his attention back to the doc. "Well, how's it lookin'?"

"Pretty good, even if I do say so myself. The toe is still bleeding some. The picric acid will encourage coagulum to form and seal the raw surfaces from infection." Doc unwrapped the bandages on Dalton's hands. Some skin from broken blisters clung to the inside of the cotton wraps.

"I was beginning to worry about you when you didn't show up by three o'clock yesterday. Billy got away, I take it?"

"Yeah. Snuck up on me in the blizzard and thumped me upside the head."

Nothing else was said while Doc inspected Dalton's blistered hands.

Then, as Doc inspected his scalp, Dalton asked, "How's my dogs?"

"Good, good. Siwash Jimmy helped Corrine feed and bed 'em down. Your hard head's gonna be alright, by the way. How's your eyesight? Blurry or anything out of the ordinary?"

"No."

"Good."

Nurse Dorothy returned with the fresh bandages and ointment and placed them on a stainless steel tray.

"Thank you, Dorothy. That will be all," Doc turned his attention back to Dalton's amputated toe.

Dalton watched the nurse walk away then asked, "Doc?"

"Yes?" Doc answered absentmindedly, as he dabbed ointment on the raw tissues of Dalton's toe.

Dalton winched a little from the pain.

"How's she doin'? She hasn't come to see me or check on me since I've been back."

Doc raised his eyebrows and glanced up at Dalton's face then back at the toe.

"She's a little upset with you...taking a fool's chance like this."

Dalton closed his eyes and briefly relived the moments before leaving to catch Billy.

"Yeah, I was in a hurry. I thought I could catch him at Lignite, but I just missed him. One thing led to another and before I knew it, I was halfway to Nenana."

Doc looked into Dalton's eyes. "That's not what I'm talking about. She's upset about your plans to face down Ward."

Dalton clenched his jaws and thought a bit as he slowly shook his head.

"Doc, Ward is bringin' this to me – not the other way around. If I... if we run, he *will* find us and it will be the same thing all over again. Sooner or later, I'm gonna have to take the bull by the tail and face the situation, and now's as good a time as any."

"You're crippled, con-sarn-it! And you ain't no spring chicken, neither. At least disappear for a while until you heal up!"

"Doc. I ain't runnin'!"

Doc turned back to inspecting Dalton's toe. "Yeah, I know. Well, we don't know where

Ward is. Could be he's nowhere near here. That would give you some time to heal up."

"Billy said it'd be a day or two."

"Could be Billy doesn't know what he's talking about or just flat out lying to you."

Dalton thought it over. "No. I saw it in his eyes. He was tellin' the truth as he knew it."

* * *

Corrine finished packing her clothes in the suitcase, and then carried it and the one with Jackson's clothes into the front room. She sat the two suitcases down and looked around the room.

She'd had high hopes for some time alone with Dalton and Jackson but those hopes all seemed to have been dashed to pieces.

Once again, the thoughts that had tormented her yesterday and robbed her of sleep last night returned. She didn't understand why Dalton couldn't just walk away, take her and Jackson someplace safe, and just be a family. *Why is he being so stubborn?* There was a good chance he wouldn't survive against four men. And the talk going around about Dalton's injuries pretty much guaranteed it.

Jackson walked into the front room carrying the black wolf carving.

"Mama, can I take this?"

The wolf carving instantly brought to mind the face of her grandfather, *Zhoh Zhraii*—black wolf in the white man's tongue—and then Bandit, Dalton's favorite lead dog, sired by a black wolf. In those days, Dalton was her only concern, her main focus in life. She was still concerned, of course, for him but now there was another she had to think about. And she was not willing to put Jackson's life in jeopardy.

"Yes, little one. Put it safe in your parka pocket."

* * *

At the stage stop, Corrine placed the two suitcases on the boardwalk. Taking Jackson by the hand, she stepped inside and asked the stage driver, "How much time do we have?"

The stage driver took out his pocket watch, looked at it and said, "About twenty minutes."

With a nod of her head, she turned and led Jackson out the door and into the cold, dark street toward the infirmary.

At the front desk, Corrine asked for directions to Dalton's room. Then, she and Jackson made their way down the hall to his door. Opening the door just enough to peer inside, she saw Dalton was awake, lying in the bed. Pushing the door open, she walked into the room, leading little Jackson by the hand.

"PAPA," Jackson exclaimed, as he ran to his father with his arms outstretched.

Corrine watched as Dalton's face lit up. He reached over to the side of the bed with his bandaged hands and hugged Jackson as he ran into his daddy's arms.

"Oh, I've missed you," Dalton said.

"You alright?" Jackson asked, as he pulled away slightly.

"Yeah, I'm alright. You been good for Mama?"

Jackson nodded his head. "Yes, I been good."

Dalton smiled and pulled Jackson up to sit by him on the bed. "That's my boy."

Corrine walked to the bedside and smiled briefly at the tenderness, love, and respect shown between a father and his son.

Then, Dalton turned to her. "It does my heart good to see you here." He reached out to her. Taking her in his arms he continued, "I was beginning to wonder if you would come to see me."

While in his embrace, Corrine closed her eyes, and thought, *This is going to be hard. How do I tell him I am leaving and taking Jackson out of here?*

Continuing to hold her close, Dalton whispered, "You feel so good in my arms. I need you so much right now."

Corrine couldn't help the little sob as tears welled up in her eyes.

Dalton released his embrace, looked at her and asked, "What is it? What's wrong?"

Corrine shrugged Dalton's bandaged hands off her shoulders and took a step back. She wiped the tears away.

"I have more to think about than just you. If you want to face Ward, then that is your business. But I am not putting our son's life in danger by staying here. We are leaving on the eight o'clock stage back to Fairbanks. It is the last stage to Nenana until spring. When this is all over, and if you are still alive, that is where you will find us."

Corrine turned to their son and held out her hand. "Jackson, come."

"But Mama..." Jackson began.

"Now!" she answered sternly.

Corrine watched as Jackson looked up at his father briefly, then back at her. A sad look came over his face as he slid off the edge of the bed.

She took him by the hand then looked back at Dalton. She could see his cheek muscles bulge as he clenched his teeth.

"I am sorry," she said.

She turned and led Jackson out the door.

CHAPTER 10

FOR TWO HOURS AFTER SHE'D left, Dalton wallowed in self-pity, self-doubt, and anger. He couldn't hobble after her because the pain in his frostbitten toes had increased since his arrival, not to mention the pain from the amputation. Even if he could, he probably wouldn't have tried. He decided she was right about one thing—this was no place for little Jackson. Nor was it any place for her. If it turned out he didn't survive this showdown, Corrine would be at Ward's mercy.

All this laying around in bed was eating on him a little. *I've got to do something*, he thought.

Feeling restless, Dalton threw the covers back, sat up on the edge of the bed, then gingerly placed his weight on his feet. Standing upright and holding onto the bed, he shuffled a couple of steps to test his balance. He was surprised to find how much losing a part of his big toe affected that balance. The pain was worse than he remembered yesterday. Of course, yesterday his feet were half-frozen and numb. Today, everything was alive and super sensitive.

I've just got to ignore it. Push it away, grit my teeth and move on, he thought. *According to Corrine, that's exactly what I've been doing most of my life. Pushin' the pain away.*

He shook his head and looked around the room. As he did so, his eyes caught his image in the mirror. He watched as a frown crossed his face. He didn't like what he saw looking back at him—a crippled old man, gray around the temples and more wrinkles than he remembered. What he remembered was a strong, younger man—a man who could find killers and horse thieves and highwaymen because of his talent as a tracker—a job he did with pride.

Dalton gritted his teeth and watched the muscles bulge along his jawline. Then he looked away. If Ward caught him like this, it'd all be over for sure. He had to get back in shape, he decided. If that meant pushing the pain away, then so be it. A few more steps and he made it to the bedside chair. Turning, he shuffled back to the bed, then back to the chair once again. Then, Dalton stopped and sat down. For fifteen minutes, he rested as the pain subsided in his toes. Then once again he made the circuit. Only this time he added more distance. From the chair to the bed, to the chair, to the bed, then back to the chair. This time the pain was less. Another short rest, then he stood up and doggedly put one foot in front of the other until he made it around the bed and back to the chair.

"I can do this," he whispered to himself.

Doc entered the room, carrying a cane.

"Up and walking around I see. That's good. I was going to suggest you start doing that. Just be careful of that toe. How ya feeling?"

Dalton turned his head and watched Doc sit down on the edge of the bed.

"It's a might painful, and I'm surprised how much I depended on my big toe for balance."

"Yeah, you never know how much you appreciate something 'til it's gone."

Dalton thought a bit. "Yeah, I been findin' that out lately..." Then, to change the subject, "Doc, I gotta get outta here. I'm all antsy bein' cooped up like this. Nobody knows for sure where Ward is, and Corrine and my son are headin' back to Fairbanks. I'm worried somethin' is going to happen."

"You're stove up. They ain't much you can do right now but wait for Ward to make his move. If you want, I can give you something for the pain, if you need it."

Dalton looked up. "Oh no! I ain't takin' any of that stuff. I can't afford dulled senses right now. I'm gonna have to keep my wits about me."

Doc frowned. "All right, then. Go home and take this cane with you. It'll help with your balance. Try to get some rest and stop worrying about Corrine. Chances are, she'll be alright."

Dalton shifted his gaze toward the window and sighed deeply. He noticed it was getting light outside. "I hope you're right."

Thirty minutes later, Dalton stepped out of the hospital door. He stopped to let his eyes adjust to the brightness of the newly risen sun, veiled behind an overcast sky. He leaned his cane against the infirmary and pulled his pocket watch from his front pants' pocket. He pushed the button on the stem and flipped open the cover. It read ten minutes after eleven.

Corrine should be about halfway to Nenana by now, he thought.

He snapped the cover closed and absent-mindedly stuffed it back into his pocket as he looked around. The cloud cover looked to be thinning some and it felt colder. His ears stung from the cold, and he flipped his hood up. Pulling on his mittens, he turned, picked up the cane, and limped toward his house. He was concerned first for his dogs, and second, that the fire had burned out in the stove, leaving the house cold.

He needn't have worried.

Upon his arrival, he found the dogs already fed and sleeping in the dog houses on beds of fresh hay, curled up with their tails covering their noses. Corrine had stoked the stove well with coal and turned the damper down so it would burn slower.

Dalton sat on a chair and watched the fire through the stove's isinglass window and thought, *She always was one to think of the details. I just wish she hadn't left me. I miss her and little Jackson.* He sighed deeply. *But she's probably right. It's best to keep our son out of danger as much as possible.*

Dalton reached over and rattled the fire grates to settle the ashes, and then pulled the ash pan. He dumped the ash into a metal bucket by the stove. After re-stoking the fire, he headed to the chow hall for lunch.

Dalton opened the chow hall door, stepped to the right, and scanned the room as his eyes adjusted to the dim interior. The usual mushers were there, but only four or five contract workers were eating. Most of the laborers had left for Fairbanks. Healy Fork was slowly becoming a ghost town for the winter. After closing the door, he removed his parka and hung it on a peg by the door.

"Don't you guys ever leave?" he asked, as he limped toward the table.

"Ain't got nuthin' to go home to," Siwash Jimmy replied.

Dalton glanced at him as he sat down and said, "Yeah, I know how that is."

"What? What are ya talkin' about? You got Corrine to go home to. Purtiest thing this side of the Yukon, if ya want my opinion."

Dalton looked over at the musher who had just spoken. It was White Moose with a questioning look on his face.

Dalton leaned forward, placed his forearms on the table, and folded his hands together. After looking at each musher in turn, he said, "Boys, she up and left me this mornin'. Took the eight-o-clock stage headin' back to Fairbanks."

Everyone sat silent. Each lost in his own thoughts.

"Well...if that's what she's done, she must have had a good reason."

Dalton looked at the speaker. It was Laughing Ollie. "Yeah, I suppose she did. She's concerned about Jackson's safety. Wants to take him back home before anythin' happens."

"Well, ya know how we all feel. Ya need to skedaddle out of here, too. Lay low for a while 'til this all blows over. Especially since you're all crippled up."

Dalton looked back at Siwash, then down to his folded hands. Shaking his head slowly, he said, "No. I can't do that. And if ya can't understand that, I can't explain it to ya."

The door flung opened and Ted, the young man from the post and telegraph office, walked in with a fog of cold air rushing along the floor. Dalton groaned inside himself. Every time Ted showed up, he was the bearer of bad news, it seemed.

"Mr. Laird?"

"Ted. Come in," Dalton said. "Now what?"

Ted closed the door, walked across the floor and handed Dalton a slip of paper. "Got a telegram fer ya. It came in a couple of hours ago."

Dalton took it and read it to himself. "Well...that answers that."

"What's it say?" White Moose asked, impatiently.

Dalton looked into the questioning eyes of Ted and the mushers. "It says Frank Ward, Paul Burkall, Indian Charlie, and Billy Smith are already in Nenana." Then, looking up at the wall and nothing in particular, said, "And Corrine and little Jackson are headin' right to 'em."

"Son-of-a...that ain't good," Siwash said as he looked down at the floor. Then looking at Dalton, asked, "Who's it from?"

Dalton shrugged his shoulders. "It just says, '*A friend*'."

Dalton suddenly stood up and hobbled to the door where his parka was hanging.

"Where ya goin'?" someone asked.

"I gotta catch up to that stage, turn it around, and bring 'em back. She's headin' into trouble," Dalton said, as he pulled the parka off the peg and struggled to pull it on.

"Oh, no you don't. You're in no condition to travel that or any other trail. Besides, she's more 'en halfway there. With your team, you'll never catch up to 'er."

Dalton turned to look at the speaker. It was White Moose.

"Got any better ideas?" Dalton growled as he continued to struggle with his parka.

"As a matter of fact, I do. One of us'll go after her. Our teams are faster. If we leave now, maybe, just maybe, we can catch up to the stage and bring 'er back."

Dalton, still struggling with the parka, bumped his toe. The pain made him grit his teeth. He seemed to hurt all over. He wanted to roar at the world in frustration. It seemed everything and everyone was against him.

Dalton pulled the parka off, wadded it up, and threw it onto the nearest table.

"Alright. Get harnessed up and take off after her."

CHAPTER 11

"WHOA, THERE," THE DRIVER CALLED out to the team, as the stage slowed to a stop in front of the two-story Nenana Roadhouse.

Corrine looked around at the bustling little community. Even though it was dark, the new electric lights shown through the storefront windows and provided a cheery glow on the snow-covered streets. There seemed to be a lot more people than there were two days ago when she was headed to Healy Fork. Most of the people paid no attention to the stage arrival. However, she noticed there were a couple of men who seemed to be curious about who was arriving. One, she noted, was a short, pudgy white man with a beard and gray wool coveralls. The other looked to be Indian.

"Help ya with your lap blanket, ma'am?"

Corrine looked toward the voice. It was the stage driver standing next to the step.

"*Aaha*, um, yes."

She lifted the edge of the fur blanket from her and Jackson and guided it toward the driver. He pulled it from the stage. Rolling it up in a ball, he tucked it under one arm and then offered his hand to help Corrine step off the stage.

"Meetin' anyone here, ma'am?"

"No. Going on to Fairbanks in the morning. We need a room for the night," she said, as she stepped down off the stage.

The driver looked around. "Well, good luck with that. Looks like all them railroad workers are gathering here at the main construction camp for Christmas."

Corrine turned and reached to help Jackson down as the driver unloaded their trunks.

As she stood Jackson on his feet on the ground, she heard someone holler, "Mrs. Laird!"

She turned and watched a dog driver break his team to a stop and stomp the snow hook into the hard-packed snow behind the stage. The dogs were panting with their tongues hanging to the side of their mouths, puffing clouds of steam. She knew they had been driven hard. *Did something happen to Dalton*, she wondered? Her heart skipped a beat.

"Mrs. Laird?" The man asked again as he stepped toward her.

"Yes."

"Dalton asked me to catch up to ya and fetch ya back to Healy Fork."

"Who are you?"

"They call me White Moose Ned, or just White Moose, ma'am."

She recognized the name. Dalton had spoken of him in the past. She noticed he was breathing heavily also, and the frost buildup on his beard, mustache, eyebrows, and fur ruff on his parka proved he had been on the trail for a while. Probably ran most of the way behind the sled.

"What's happened?"

Stepping closer, he said in a hushed voice, "Dalton got a telegram that this Ward fella is here in Nenana. He thinks you're in danger."

Anger flooded her veins. With a raised voice she said, "First off, my son and I just spent ten hours on that stage."

Moose took a step back.

"We are cold and hungry and tired. I am not going to ride that sled for another five or six hours back to Healy. I am going to get a room, if there is any, and take care of my son." Glancing at the dogs, she continued in a lowered voice, "Besides, you and the dogs need rest, also."

Staring wide-eyed at her, White Moose stammered, "Um...yes, ma'am. Mm... maybe in the mornin'?"

"I will think on it."

She watched as White Moose mounted his sled, pulled the snow hook, and headed to the dog livery. Her heart felt heavy. She regretted unleashing her anger on him. After all, he was just delivering a message. At times like this, she reminded herself of her father, and she did not like it.

Reaching down, she took Jackson by the hand and turned toward the boardwalk of the Nenana Roadhouse. As she did so, she looked for the two men across the street. They were still there. One watched the stage. The other watched as White Moose drove his team to the dog livery.

Corrine stepped into the lobby of the roadhouse with a rush of cold air rolling along the floor, and a fog of warm moist air rushing upward out of the door and into the dark, frigid arctic night.

The place was crowded with working men and women all talking at once and eating supper or playing card games. Jackson clung to his mother's leg as she worked to get the door closed.

Glancing around the lobby, she noticed the stage passenger she had ridden with from Fairbanks two days before—the man with the brown Bowler hat. They made eye contact and he smiled briefly and tipped his hat to her. She located the check-in desk, then picked up Jackson and held him in her arms as she made her way through the crowd.

At the desk stood the proprietor.

"Help ya?"

"I need a room for the night."

He chuckled a little, then said, "All my rooms are full up. Ever bodies full up. Most my rooms upstairs, I got five men sharing."

As Corrine considered her options, she felt the presence of someone standing beside her but she ignored it. After all, the room *was* crowded.

"You must have someplace my son and I can spend the night."

The proprietor opened his mouth to speak but was cut off by a voice at her side. "Mrs. Laird?"

She turned to the voice. It was the man in the Bowler hat.

"If you will permit me, ma'am. You and the boy there can have my room for the night. It's um... it's private."

"Who are you?"

"I um... I work for the railroad, ma'am."

Corrine frowned, and then said, "A lot of people work for the railroad."

The proprietor interrupted, "Ma'am, I wouldn't look a gift horse in the mouth. It's the best you're gonna find."

Corrine glanced at the owner, then back at the man with the Bowler hat.

It would be better than trying to sleep in the lobby or the hay of the livery stables, she thought. It seemed she had no other option.

"Alright."

"Good. I'll grab your trunks and you can follow me."

Bowler hat man hefted Corrine's trunk to his right shoulder and balanced it there with his right hand. With his left, he picked up Jackson's smaller trunk by the handle.

He negotiated his way through the crowd and up the narrow stairway. Corrine and Jackson stayed close behind, and she noticed several men duck out of the way to let Bowler hat man and her, carrying little Jackson, through. One of the men looked like the Indian she had seen leaning against the porch post across the street earlier but she wasn't sure.

At the end of the hallway, Bowler hat man stopped at the last room on the left. She noticed there was a door on the outside wall at the end of the hallway, which presumably led to an outside stairway.

Bowler hat man sat the trunks down, unlocked the door, and stepped back to allow her and Jackson to enter. As she looked around, Bowler hat man carried the trunks into the room. Everything was neat and clean. Clothes were folded neatly on the dresser, and the bed was made.

Bowler hat man must have seen the surprised look on her face.

"I, um...I had good upbringing. That and some army discipline."

Corrine turned directly toward him and watched him close the door, then asked, "Who *are* you?"

He reached into the breast pocket of his vest and produced a badge and identification. "Charles Daily, ma'am. I um... I work for the Pinkerton Detective Agency."

"You said you worked for the railroad," she said, as she glanced at the badge.

Daily motioned for her to sit down on the bed while he took a seat on the one chair in the room. Taking off his hat, he leaned forward and placed both elbows on his knees. He held his hat in his hands.

"Um... no, ma'am. I uh... well, that's what I tell people. You see, this is a federal project, and, well, the agency can't work for the federal government, not since the Anti-Pinkerton Act in 93. No...no, I work for a private mining company up in the Fortymile district."

Corrine thought a bit. "So, what are you doing here?"

"Well, ma'am... now that's where it gets interesting. I'm after this here Paul Burkall feller. Se...seems as though he tried to organize the workers of the mining company... you know, for higher wages and such... Well, I was hired to break it up. But before I could get there, Burkall got involved in a ruckus, you see, and... Well, he shot somebody."

Corrine recalled hearing Dalton mention the name.

"Anyhow..." Daily continued, "I, uh, I was in Fairbanks at the marshal's office, you see, when word came in about Indian Charlie and Frank Ward possibly being in Circle City, accompanied by a man who fit Burkall's description. Well, the marshal filled me in on Ward and your husband's past."

"White Moose, a dog musher my husband knows, just told me that they were all in town."

Daily looked up at her, nodded his head and said, "Yes, ma'am, they are."

"So why have you not arrested them or whatever?"

Daily frowned then looked back at his hat as he slowly turned it around in his hands.

"Well, ma'am, I uh... well, I'm only interested in Burkall... ma'am, and there's four of them and, well, one against four isn't very good odds. No... no, I figure I'll follow them on to Healy Fork. I figure your husband and I could handle two apiece... if need be."

Corrine looked over at Jackson playing with the carved black wolf and thought about what Daily was saying. Then she thought about Dalton, all crippled up. Hardly anybody was left in Healy Fork to help him. And those who were still there didn't want anything to do with his fight. She didn't either, for that matter. Even she had left him, and she felt guilty about it. But she had Jackson to think about—she could never forgive herself if anything happened to him. Of course, if something happened to Dalton, she knew she could never forgive herself for that either. Should she go back?

Looking back at Daily she said, "My husband wants us back in Healy so he can protect us from Ward. That is why White Moose was here. To take us back."

Daily glanced at her. "You asking my opinion, ma'am?"

"*Aaha$_i$'*."

Daily sat upright in the chair and looked at the floor a bit. Then, looking at her he said, "Well... ma'am, that's a hard one. There's going to be trouble, sure as shootin', and I wouldn't want to see a lady and her child caught up in the middle of it. But a man needs a woman to stand by him through the hard times and the good. Even if she doesn't understand him. From what I know of your husband, ma'am, he is a man of honor. He has a professional duty to the citizens of this territory to put an end to Ward and the lingering effect of your father's influence.

"I'm sure he's feeling abandoned right now...and torn. Torn between needing you there with him like you were years ago in that cabin fighting your father and the syndicate, but also hoping you and his son get away safe, if he has to pay the ultimate sacrifice."

She remembered that cabin and the gunfight they'd had with her father and his gang.

"I, uh... I'm sure he's concerned about your safety, first and foremost. Since you're already here, I, um... I'll make sure you get on that stage and out of town safely, back to Fairbanks in the morning. I'll send a message to him to let him know. Wo... would that be alright, ma'am?"

Corrine looked over at little Jackson still playing with the black wolf carving. She thought of her grandfather, and Bandit, Dalton's lead dog sired by a black wolf. She remembered those days when love was new. With the help of Yukon Jack, she had left everything to be with Dalton. To take care of him. To be his helpmate.

She suddenly knew what she must do.

CHAPTER 12

FRANK WARD AND BURKALL SAT at the Faro table in the back of the Frostbite Saloon on one of the back streets of Nenana. Gambling was officially forbidden in the AEC construction camps, however, no one seemed to be enforcing regulations during the holidays.

Ward had just laid down a winning hand and was raking in the pile when Indian Charlie, standing at the bar, caught Ward's eye. Ward felt anger seethe inside. He was on a winning streak and he regretted having to leave the table. However, he knew Charlie would never bother him unless he thought it was important.

"Boys... the time has come for me to take my leave. And it's been a pleasure taking your money."

Amid groans of protest from those who had lost the most, Ward stacked the bills, stood up, and stuffed them into his pants' pocket.

Picking up his drink, he turned and made his way to Indian Charlie.

"What's going on?" Ward leaned both elbows against the bar next to Charlie.

"Woman in town."

Ward gritted his teeth. It always irritated him trying to get information out of Charlie.

Ward turned his head and looked at Charlie. "There's lots of women in town."

"She come from south, on stage."

Ward looked back at his drink and slowly rolled the glass between his palms. *Could it be Corrine?* he wondered.

Looking back at Charlie he asked, "Do you think it's...*her*?"

Indian Charlie shrugged. "She half-breed, with child."

Ward smiled. It seemed his luck was still holding.

Charlie continued. "White mans follow on empty dog sled."

Ward caught his breath, and then looked back at his drink between his palms as he rolled it back and forth. *It could be Dalton*, he thought. *But why would he be following by dog sled? Why not ride the stage?*

"Know who it is?" Ward asked as he sipped his drink.

"Heard name. White Moose. They argue. He go to dog livery. She go to roadhouse."

"Where's Billy?"

"He follow White Moose to dog livery. I follow woman."

Ward tossed back the last of the drink and sat it on the bar. "Find Billy. Bring him to our room at the roadhouse."

Ward turned and made eye contact with Burkall, still at the table playing his hand. Ward nodded his head toward the door and left.

* * *

Twenty minutes later, they were all assembled in the small room the four men shared at the Nenana Roadhouse. Ward watched Indian Charlie squatting in the corner of the room with his back to the wall, slowly building a cigarette.

"You said Corrine came here. Where is she? Fill us in on the details." Then, looking around the room, added, "And the rest of you, keep it down. These walls are thin."

Ward looked back at Charlie, but Charlie didn't answer. He rolled the paper stuffed with tobacco into a cylinder and licked the edge to glue it down. Again, Ward felt the familiar anger seethe inside. Sometimes it seemed Charlie deliberately procrastinated just to irritate him. *Didn't he understand the importance of this information?* Ward felt his anger turn to a simmer and was about to open his mouth to chastise Charlie when Indian Charlie looked up at him.

"I follow her inside. She no can find place to sleep. Man in Bowler hat give her his room."

Charlie turned his attention back to matters at hand and struck a match on the floor. He lit the cigarette, exhaled, and looked back at Ward through a cloud of nicotine.

"So, where *is* she, Charlie?"

Charlie blew out the match. "At end of hall, left side, by outside stairway."

Ward felt the anger die down as the thought crossed his mind, *Finally. After all these years, Corrine Batiste* (as he knew her) *is within reach. But what about this dandy with the Bowler hat? Who is he anyway? He always seems to be there, just inside the shadows.*

Ward looked at Smith and Burkall. "Know anything about this dandy in the Bowler hat?"

Both shook their heads.

Ward looked back at Charlie, who had just taken a drag from his cigarette. Charlie exhaled and said, "He big shot with railroad. He stay at AEC dormitory tonight."

A smile crossed Ward's face. "Seems as though lady luck is still with us, boys."

Looking at Indian Charlie, he said, "I want you to take care of this Moose fella." Then, looking around at the others, he continued, "We'll get some sleep. Be ready at six in the mornin'. You three get White Moose's team and Smith's dogs along with another team from the livery. Meet me at the bottom of the back stairs. I'll have Corrine and the kid. It's time to visit Mr. Dalton Laird."

Indian Charlie crushed out his cigarette, rose, and slipped out the door and down the hall. Ward followed him just to the door and leaned against the jamb. Looking down the hallway, he could see light coming from underneath the door of the last room on the left by the outside stairway.

A shadow moved in the light.

He smiled.

Burkall stepped up beside him. "Why not do it now?"

Ward continued to gaze at the light under the door. "If we leave now, we'll get there too soon. I want to be there at sunup so I can plainly see the look on Dalton's face when he realizes I have his woman... and that he's gonna die."

CHAPTER 13

CORRINE HAD BEEN ON THE trail for three hours with White Moose Ned's dogs when she finally stopped the team and set the snow hook. From the way the dogs' tongues lolled to the side, she could tell they were overheated and needed a break. The frost build-up from their heavy panting in the frigid subarctic air coated their muzzles and chest. She had run the dogs hard, trying to put distance and time between her son and her, and what they left behind. She needed a break, as well, for she had run most of the way behind the sled trying to lighten the dogs' load.

After shaking the frost buildup caused by her heavy breathing from the wolverine ruff on her parka hood, she tossed the hood back and listened into the deafening quiet. Deciding that all was well, Corrine then checked on little Jackson—fast asleep and bundled inside the fur blanket in the sled basket. As she gazed at him, she wondered again if she'd made the right decision.

While talking last night with Mr. Dailey, the Pinkerton man, she'd come to realize some things. First, that her place was by Dalton's side, shoulder-to-shoulder, come what may. She'd been selfish leaving Dalton. There are things more important than self and she hoped he would forgive her. She loved Dalton for his strength and honor. His strong sense of right and wrong. Not just for the family alone, but the community and the land. Something her father never possessed.

Second, she had realized the safest place in the world for her and their son was with Dalton.

And third, because of the two men who had been watching the stage, she knew for certain Ward was aware of her presence and that something was about to happen. So, she decided the sooner she left for Healy Fork, the better.

Yes, she decided again, *I made the right decision.*

She had lain awake for hours after her talk with Mr. Dailey thinking on those things until finally, feeling restless, she knew she couldn't wait any longer. With little Jackson still clutching his carved black wolf, she bundled him up in a fur blanket and snuck down the outside stairway. She then hurried to the dog livery hoping to find White Moose to take them back to Healy Fork. Instead, she found his body half-hidden under some straw in the back of the livery with his throat cut.

She quickly harnessed the dogs and draped half of a tanned caribou hide in the basket of the sled, hair side up. On this, she gently placed little Jackson, still wrapped in the fur blanket. Over this bundle, she draped the other half of the caribou hide and tucked under the edges. The bundle was lashed down to the stanchions to keep it in place.

She looked around for some kind of weapon Moose surely must have carried, but the only thing she found was a sheath knife. This, she had tied around her waist under her parka.

As she squatted beside the sled, she felt the heft of the knife and it brought her comfort.

Corrine looked around.

A waning gibbous moon in the last quarter had risen last night at 11:00. It glowed overhead and the clear, crisp subarctic night allowed all of its light to reach the snow-covered ground. This, in turn, reflected in all directions with a diffused light. The northern lights added their glow of blues, yellows, and greens. They danced across the firmament in waves, like the rippling of a great flag in the breeze. The visibility was good.

She'd stopped the dogs on an incline where the railroad right-of-way begins its climb toward the Alaska Range. Her back trail lead out onto the muskeg flats that ran back to Nenana. From her vantage point, she could see for several miles. To her left, she noticed a brush pile that had been burned, evidently within the last couple of days.

As she watched and waited, she gazed at the dancing lights and thought she heard faint voices—whispering really. She remembered one of the stories her grandfather, Black Wolf—*Zhoh Zhraii*, in her mother's language—had told her when she was a little girl. He had said that the lights were the spirits of their ancestors coming back to visit.

Could it be? Was she hearing their voices? She really didn't know.

She pulled back the wolverine fur from her ears and slowly turned her head from side to side, to hear more clearly. Soon, she heard the voices again. More distinct, urgent. Her heart leapt in her chest.

"Ward," she said aloud. The name tasted bitter on her tongue.

She swiftly stood and moved to the rear of the sled. The dogs sensed her urgency and they rose from their beds, shook the snow from their coats, and leaned into their harnesses.

Corrine stood on the break, pulled the snow hook and gave the command, "Hike!"

An hour-and-a-half later, Corrine passed

Lignite. As the team made a turn in the trail, she noticed the lead dog's ears go erect, indicating something up ahead in the trail in the dark shadows interested him.

Corrine stood on the brake and stopped the team. Something big and dark suddenly ambled out of the taiga and onto the trail. A cow moose.

"Mama?" Jackson asked tentatively.

"Quiet son, lay still," she responded in a hushed voice.

"What's the matter?"

"Just a moose in the trail. Now keep quiet."

Corrine knew that during periods of deep snow, travelers sometimes had trouble with moose on the trail who didn't want to yield the right-of-way to anyone. The hard-packed trail provided easy access to food. Coupled with the fact that moose and canines have been rivals for millennia, and that moose have a difficult time fighting wolves in deep snow, they sometimes choose to stand and fight.

This one chose to fight.

Corrine saw the moose lower her head and the hackles rise along her neck. Then, the cow swung its head from side to side. Corrine heard her make a rumbling growl.

My baby!

Corrine jumped to the side of the sled, reached over the side rail, and desperately worked the lashing that held little Jackson in his warm cocoon. The dogs bolted forward to meet the cow. The sled knocked Corrine off-balance but she was able to grab the side rail. The moving sled dragged her about ten feet before it stopped.

Jackson cried.

Corrine heard the whimpering, growls, anguished howling, and shrieks of wounded dogs as the cow moose and dogs clashed in mortal combat. After regaining her footing, she again feverishly worked at the knot. *If only I'd used a highwayman's hitch*, as Dalton had taught her. *Too late for that now*.

"Jackson, stop crying," she hissed. Jackson stopped crying but continued to whimper.

Glancing to her left, she could see the cow moose kicking and stomping among the tethered team. In their attempt to save their own lives, frustrated dogs snarled and snapped at anything that got in their way, including each other. Corrine knew if the fight got any closer to the sled, she and her son would be slashed to pieces.

Turning her attention back to Jackson, she finally got the knot untied. Lifting Jackson out of the sled, Corrine desperately looked around for a safe place away from flailing hooves and slashing teeth of enraged huskies.

A tree, she thought. *Get behind a tree!*

Quickly scanning the darkened forest, she spotted a big spruce standing about fifteen feet from her. Standing up, she cradled her son to her breast and lunged off the trail and into the deep snow. She sank halfway up her thighs.

Lifting one snow-entombed foot high, she took a step forward and sunk it back down into the snow.

Laboriously, she pulled the other snow-entombed foot high and took another step forward. Only twelve more feet and she would be at the spruce.

Looking over her shoulder in desperation, she saw the cow moose had turned its attention on her and was coming for her, paying no attention to the dogs snarling at its feet.

Corrine screamed and Jackson started crying again. She fixed her attention back on the relative safety of the spruce tree.

I have to make it to that tree.

She took another laborious step forward. Then another. She looked back. The moose was off the trail and coming fast.

I'll never make it, she decided.

What could she do? She could shield Jackson's body from the slashing hooves with hers.

"Quiet son. I need you to stop crying."

With a sob, Corrine pulled Jackson tightly to her breast and fell forward in the snow.

Buried in their tomb of ice crystals, she heard a muffled explosion, and another, and felt a mild shockwave through the snow. She lay still, listening, waiting for the deadly blows of the enraged moose.

Nothing happened.

From under the snow, she heard dogs snarling and fighting. *Did the moose turn back on the dogs?* She wondered.

Faintly, far off, she thought she heard voices.

"Womans here."

"You two, take care of those dogs."

Corrine felt herself being yanked up from the snow that had enshrouded her and Jackson. Fear turned to intense anger at the thought of anything harming her son, and she struck out at the moose with her free hand.

As the snow fell away from her vision, she realized it wasn't a moose after all. It was an Indian—the man she had seen in Nenana watching the stage. He had a surprised look on his face as four ugly scratches that crossed his cheek and nose began welling blood.

"I told ya she's a wildcat!"

Corrine turned and looked toward the voice. It was Frank Ward.

Quickly looking around herself, she saw the moose lying dead and half-buried in the snow, not five feet from her. Two gunshots pierced the night and the anguished howling of mortally wounded huskies ceased.

Corrine snapped her head in the direction of the gunshots and watched two men unhook two limp bodies from the gangline and toss the dead dogs off the trail.

"Guess Burkall had to put two of 'em out of their misery."

Corrine looked back at Ward.

"You all right?" he asked.

"*Aaha҆'*."

She looked over at Indian Charlie. He held a handful of pink snow to the four gashes across his face. There was hate in his eyes.

"I safe your life. I kill moose. You do this to me."

Corrine had known from the beginning he was not Athabascan. Looking closer, she decided he was Cree. As such, he probably didn't know Athabascan but he may know some of the Chinook Jargon trade language—a language made up of a mish-mash of English, French, and several Indian languages that had evolved over the last couple hundred years but was fast disappearing.

Corrine thought a bit, recalling some of the words she'd learned as a child, as she comforted a still-fussing Jackson. Perhaps she could appease his anger and appeal to his cultural background.

Looking at Charlie, she said, "*Me-si'-ka wau'-wau Chinook la-lang?*"

Charlie straightened up a bit and looked at her intently. "Ah-ha."

"*Sick tum'-tum. Me-si'-ka skoo'-kum tum'-tum man. Mah-sie.*"

Indian Charlie looked her up and down and then looked at the handful of bloody snow. This, he threw to the ground, nodded once to her, then turned and waded through the snow back to the trail.

"What was that all about?" Ward growled.

Corrine smiled to herself as she looked back at Ward. "I asked him if he spoke the Chinook language. He said 'yes' so I told him I felt bad and thanked him."

Of course, she didn't tell him that she had also said she thought he was a strong warrior.

Wards' eyes narrowed. "Yeah, well from now on you speak English around my men, ya hear? Now get yourself up to the trail. We're headin' to Healy Fork."

CHAPTER 14

DALTON SAT DOWN AT THE table in his house with a mug of hot tea crooked in his wrapped trigger finger. Setting the mug on the table, he fumbled for a tea-ball and a bag of finely chopped willow bark. Placing some of the bark in the tea-ball, Dalton added that to the hot tea and absentmindedly lifted it up and down, steeping the goodness out of the bark.

Humans had been using willow bark for thousands of years to reduce pain, and Dalton preferred it to the stupefying effects of the opioids Doc wanted to prescribe. Dalton took a sip. It was bitter.

Sitting there alone, he thought again about Corrine's leaving and he felt the weight of the world on his shoulders. Dalton didn't begrudge Corrine's decision. He understood her concern for Jackson's safety. He was hurt though, because of her lack of understanding of his sense of duty—that this was something he couldn't walk away from. Hopefully, they were safely on the stage somewhere between Nenana and Fairbanks.

The throbbing in his foot brought his mind back to his own well-being. Because of a hasty decision, he was now missing part of a big toe. It was like every heartbeat was trying to pump life into something that was no longer there. He realized the throbbing didn't seem as intense.

A couple of hours before, Doc had drained the blisters, leaving the dead skin attached to help seal the raw flesh from infection. Then he added some kind of ointment and re-wrapped his fingers one by one, lightly, so Dalton could use his hands. Specifically, his trigger finger.

Dalton took another sip of tea. Looking around the empty house, he suddenly felt all alone, once again. Siwash Jimmy had vol- unteered to take a load of mail to Talkeetna. There was an Indian girl and her family there he wanted to spend Christmas with. Laughing Ollie had suddenly decided to travel with him. There was some land in the Matanuska Valley he was thinking of homesteading.

The chow hall cook was busy closing up the kitchen for the winter, and Doc and his nurse, Dorothy, were packing to leave for Fairbanks. In a day or two, the only other people left in the construction camp of Healy Fork would be the telegraph and post office manager and

Ted, his helper. They would be visited by an occasional freighter or musher hauling mail through the rest of the long, lonely winter's night until spring once again returned.

Loneliness.

In his younger days, which didn't seem all that long ago, he welcomed it. Back then it was a friend. A refuge. A constant. It never changed. You knew what to expect. It didn't hurt you like people did. It never abandoned you.

Then Corrine came along and pulled him out of the loneliness and into a world he had secretly longed for—the love of a good woman, a family, and all that it means.

He hated the loneliness now and knew he could never go back.

Someone knocked on his door.

"Come in," Dalton hollered.

The door opened and Ted stepped in and closed the door behind himself.

"Oh, there you are. Got another telegram fer ya."

Dalton took it, opened it, and read,

WIFE AND SON HEADING TO HEALY BY DOG TEAM.

WITNESSES SAY 5 A.M.

WARD AND COMPANY CLOSE BEHIND.

WHITE MOOSE DEAD.

SIGNED: A FRIEND

A flood of mixed emotions swirled in Dalton's brain.

He was happy she was returning to him but then he was concerned for her and Jackson's safety on the trail.

Then anger, as Ward was apparently attempting to chase her down. Then, sorrow for the loss of a good friend.

Confusion as to who this *friend* was and how he fit into all this. And, anxiety. Should he harness up the team and head out to intercept her? *She's a good dog driver, and savvy.* He knew she could make it on her own. *But what about Ward? What if he caught up to her?*

Dalton had no doubt what Ward would do. He'd use her as a hostage to get to him.

What time is it? he wondered.

Dalton pulled out his pocket watch and mashed the stem. The cover popped open and revealed ten minutes to ten. Dalton looked at the telegram again. The timestamp read 7:25 a.m. If she left at five this morning, then she could be here any time now.

Dalton gritted his teeth and dropped the pocket watch on the table. Wadding the telegram in his large fist, he stood up and shook it in Ted's face.

With an even, steady tone through clenched teeth, he said, "This telegram came in two-and-a-half hours ago. Why am I just now getting it?"

He saw Ted's eyes widen as he took a step back and opened his mouth as if to speak, but no words came out.

"SPEAK TO ME, BOY!"

Ted's mouth moved a couple of times with no words, then, finally, "We... we had a lot of mail and... I tried to find... Gee, Mr. Laird, I didn't mean ..." Ted's eyes filled with tears.

Dalton closed his eyes and sighed deeply, letting the anger go. In his anger, he had forgotten Ted was still a child in his mind. In the background, he could hear Ted still talking between his sobs.

"...I'm sorry Mr. Laird. Really, I am. I'll make it up to you. I swear I will."

Dalton opened his eyes and tossed the wadded-up telegram on the table. "Ted, Ted I'm sorry. I shouldn't have gotten mad at ya. It's not your fault. There's a lot of stuff goin' on in my head and I took it out on you. I'm sorry."

Ted's crying turned to sniffles.

Sticking out his hand to Ted, Dalton asked, "Friends?"

Ted wiped his eyes on his sleeve, looked at Dalton's outstretched hand, then into Dalton's eyes. He smiled.

"Friends," he said, as he shook Dalton's hand. Then, pointing toward the crumpled telegram, asked, "Bad news?"

"I'm afraid so. Ted, listen to me. In a little while, there's gonna be some bad men come into this camp. I want you and your boss to stay inside by the telegraph. Whatever happens, don't come out. Ya hear? I don't want ya gettin' hurt."

"But..."

"No 'buts' Ted. Now go."

CHAPTER 15

"WHOA, THERE," WARD COMMANDED, AS he stood on the brake of the sled. He stopped the team on a little rise just north of Healy Fork and took out his binoculars. The sun was just coming up in the south-southeast over the Alaska Range. Holding his breath to avoid fogging the eyepiece as he brought them up to his face, he studied the layout of the little AEC construction camp.

The camp was built on the west bank of the frozen Nenana River, just across from the mouth of the Healy River. Coal bunkers lined the bank of the Nenana. Just in front of them, facing west toward the railroad right-of-way, stood a line of tents and frame buildings. One, two-story building appeared to be a hotel or boarding house. Across the right-of-way facing the boarding house stood a frame building with electric lights shining through the window. Smoke rolled from the chimney. It appeared to be the telegraph office.

Other than that, the place looked deserted.

Hearing footsteps then a voice ask, "Whatcha thinkin'," Ward lowered the binoculars and exhaled. He felt the slow burn of anger grow. Turning to the other three men who had gathered behind him, he looked at Billy Smith and asked, "You sure Dalton's in this camp?"

"He was two days ago."

Turning back to his sled, he yanked the fur blanket back. Jackson began crying. Corrine looked up at him and he saw fear in her eyes.

"Shut that kid up! Is Dalton in this camp?" he asked.

Corrine tried to console Jackson, but he would have none of it.

Ward felt the anger grow a little more intense. "Answer my question!"

Jackson thrashed around and it seemed to Ward Corrine was stalling, using Jackson as an excuse for not answering. "Gi'me that kid," he reached down and pulled Jackson out of her arms. Jackson squirmed and cried, reaching back to his mother. Corrine came up out of the sled basket. Ward saw the fear in her eyes replaced with hate.

"Yes! He is here. And you will wish he was not before the day is through!"

"Thank you," He handed Jackson back to her. Then, he noticed something black fall out of Jackson's parka pocket and land on the white snow. Picking it up, he looked at it. It was a carving of a wolf.

"That's mine! Gi'me," Jackson cried as he reached his hand out for it.

Ward smiled at Jackson and he turned the carving around in his fingers. "You be a good boy and maybe I'll give it back. But for now..." Ward stuffed the carving deep into his pocket, "I think I'll keep it."

Jackson's cry deepened as Ward turned back to his men. "Charlie, here's what I want you to do..."

* * *

Dalton had just finished cleaning his Colt 1911 .45. After working the slide a couple of times to make sure everything was working, he locked it in the 'open' position and inserted a full magazine. Pulling back on the slide to unlock it, he let the slide go so it would return to battery with a round in the chamber. Dalton released the magazine and replaced the round with a fresh one, so that the Colt held a full magazine plus one in the chamber. He placed the Colt in his shoulder holster lying on the table.

Dalton began to load more rounds in another seven-round magazine. His wolf-dogs suddenly howled in the dog yard behind the house. Something had risen their interest. Dalton rose, leaned forward, and rubbed the heel of his bandaged hand to melt the ice on the frost-covered windowpane, then peered through it.

Dalton watched as two dog teams trotted down the street, coming from the north. One man rode in the basket as another drove the sled of the first team.

The second team only had a driver. By all reports, there were supposed to be four men. *What happened to the fourth?* he wondered. It had been a few years, but Dalton instantly recognized the tall, skinny one driving the second sled. It was Frank Ward.

The condition of the dogs caught his attention. The dogs had frozen blood on their fur and several of them limped badly. He suddenly realized it was White Moose's team and it looked to be two or three dogs short. There was no sign of Corrine.

What had happened? She was supposed to be on the trail ahead of them. Then, his jaws tightened. *Had they caught up to her? Why was there blood all over the dogs?*

Dalton looked down at the half-loaded magazine in his hand and realized twelve rounds had better be enough because he didn't have time to load more.

Reaching for his parka hanging by the door, he thought better of it and grabbed his lighter-weight canvas anorak instead.

Over this, he fastened his shoulder holster and belt. Worn on the outside, it provided quicker access to the pistol. He shoved the extra magazine into the front pocket.

Dalton stepped out of his house, shoved a martin-fur hat on his head and pulled the flaps down over his ears. Looking down the street, he could see the teams had stopped in front of the now-empty, two-story boarding house. Two figures rapidly unharnessed the dogs and turned them loose. Apparently, they didn't plan on leaving anytime soon.

The hard-packed snow squeaked under Dalton's rubber-soled snowpacks as he hastened toward the building. Blue smoke from a just-made fire belched from the smokestack. Dalton watched as one person went inside while the other unloaded some duffel bags from the sleds and carried them inside. Dalton drew his gun and took that opportunity to quicken his steps to get closer to the boarding house before being spotted.

Making it to the corner of the building, he climbed onto the porch and glanced into the window—assessing the situation. If he burst through the door with guns blazing, and Corrine and Jackson happened to be in there, she and Jackson could get hurt. He counted three men.

Dalton saw one of them turn and head for the front door. Dalton took a step back from the window. The door opened. Billy Smith stepped out onto the porch and took two steps toward the sleds. Billy suddenly stopped with his back to Dalton. Dalton could tell by Billy's movement that his hands were fumbling with something.

In a low, even tone, Dalton said, "Don't even try it, Billy. You're under arrest. Now back up toward my voice."

Billy spun around. Dalton saw a pistol in his hand.

Dalton fired two rounds center of mass. Billy crumpled to the porch.

A gun blazed from the darkened interior through the front window.

Dalton felt something tug his anorak and shards of glass and wood splinters from the windowsill peppered his face.

Overwhelmed with firepower, Dalton ducked, took one large step, and jumped off the porch. He half-ran, half-limped to the nearest building up the street. He made it around the corner just as two bullets whizzed past his head.

Leaning there against the building, he became aware of a throbbing pain in his toe from running. His fingers stiffened from the cold. Dismissing the pain in his toe, he shifted the Colt to his left hand. He shoved his gun hand under the anorak and down the front of his pants to keep his hand and, more importantly, his trigger finger warm. Peeking around the corner to see if he was being followed, he took a quick look around, figuring on what to do next.

The post and telegraph office sat directly across the street from the boarding house. Dalton saw Ted peeking out the window.

If I could make it across the street and behind the buildings, he thought, *...then work my way back to the post and telegraph office, I would have a clear view of the hotel and be able to send a telegram to Marshal Brenneman about what's going on.*

Dalton pulled his hand out from underneath his anorak and shifted the Colt to that hand. Taking a quick breath, Dalton sprinted across the street.

* * *

"Burkall, you're a little too quick with that gun," Ward began. "I told ya Dalton is mine to deal with. You coulda killed him just then."

Burkall turned from the window and looked over at Ward.

Ward's face was red and Burkall wasn't sure if it was from the cold or if anger was seething inside.

He decided it was anger, and he knew better than to push his luck.

"Sorry. I get jittery when someone starts shootin'. Especially him. I've heard stories."

Ward remained silent for a couple of moments and some color drained from his face. The answer seemed to appease him.

Burkall heard footsteps running down the stairs, then stop. He and Ward turned and saw Indian Charlie looking into the lobby.

"It's okay, Charlie. Get back up there with the squaw and the kid. And keep 'er tied up," Ward said.

Turning back to Burkall he continued, "I want ya to slip out the back and work your way up the street. Find 'im and bring 'im back. Alive. Got that?"

"Yes, sir."

Burkall headed for the back door, opened it, and cautiously peeked around the door jamb—in both directions—before exiting. He knew Dalton had headed north up the street before ducking behind the nearest building. He knew because he'd fired a couple of hasty shots at Dalton just as he disappeared behind the corner. He doubted any had connected.

With gun in hand, Burkall swiftly made his way to the back corner of the next building. He peeked around the corner just in time to see Dalton reach the building across the street. He watched as Dalton slipped around the corner and disappear. He seemed to be limping.

Perhaps I nicked Dalton with a round after all, he thought. *If so, it'll slow him down.*

Burkall ran hard across the street, slammed up against the building, and watched the corner to his left where Dalton had disappeared. Dalton didn't show. Burkall peeked around the corner.

Dalton was gone.

Hurrying to the back corner, he scanned the back of the buildings. He witnessed Dalton enter the back door of the telegraph and post office. Burkall smiled. Dalton was fairly trapped, if Ward was on his game. All he had to do was bust through the back door and take Dalton by surprise. If Dalton escaped out the front, Ward would have him covered.

Burkall tested the doorknob. It wasn't locked.

Shoving the door open, Burkall burst through the door and into the large, inner office. There Dalton stood, looking through the front window toward the boarding house. A younger man looked up from sorting mail, and an older, balding man was at the telegraph desk, clicking away.

Dalton spun and reached for his pistol.

"Don't even try it," Burkall said, as he leveled his gun at Dalton. "You do and yer a dead man."

CHAPTER 16

BURKALL STOOD WITH HIS GUN leveled at Dalton, amused at how easy it'd been to get the drop on someone with Dalton's reputation, when he heard the unmistakable four clicks of a Colt Single Action Army revolver being cocked behind his head.

"Not so fast, Burkall."

Burkall froze and saw Dalton draw his pistol and point it at him. It appeared to Burkall that Dalton was just as surprised as he.

"Who're you?" Burkall asked the voice behind his head.

"Yeah, That's what I'd like to know," Dalton said.

"Charles Daily, Pinkerton Detective Agency at your service and you're under arrest, Burkall. Now, lay that pistol down on the table, easy-like, or I will decorate the wall with the contents of your head. And if you've got half as much brains as I think you do, you'll do as I say."

Burkall calculated his chances and decided they didn't add up.

Taking his finger out of the trigger guard, he lowered the gun to the table and raised his hands head-high.

He heard the Colt SAA behind him being un-cocked and placed in its holster, then the click of a lightweight chain. Dalton still had his gun leveled at him.

"How'd you get the drop on me?" Burkall asked Daily.

"Well, I had just made the turn onto the main street and saw you running across the street like you were after somebody. So, I swung the dogs in behind a tent and watched you enter this building, gun in hand. I just followed in right behind you. You gotta learn to watch your back trail, son. Now, put your right arm behind your back."

Burkall complied, and he felt cold steel click around his wrist.

"Mind telling me why *you're* after *me*?" Burkall asked.

"Not at all. Now give me your other arm."

Burkall obliged and again, felt the cold steel.

"Remember that, uh...that little ruckus you started in the mines up in the Fortymile country? When you tried to organize the miners against the company?"

Burkall turned his head and looked at Daily. "What about it?"

"Well...oh, um, back up to that roof support post there, son."

Burkall backed up to the post and felt Daily loop a short chain through his cuffed hands and around the post. He watched Dalton re-holster his gun as Daily locked the ends of the chain with a padlock.

Burkall slid down the support pole and sat on the floor. Looking up at Daily he asked, "Well?"

"Oh...Yeah, well, I was brought in to break it up...you see, but you ended up shooting a fella before I got there and..."

"He die?"

"No...no he didn't die. But the mining company wants you to stand trial for attempted murder."

Burkall looked over at Dalton and asked, "What about you? I saw ya limping after I fired at you. Did I nick you?"

Dalton looked at him and frowned. "Didn't even come close. It's frostbite."

Burkall looked down at the floor between his knees and slowly shook his head. "Dang!" he said. "Seems I can't shoot straight."

* * *

During the last part of the conversation between Burkall and Daily, Dalton had been wondering about Corrine and little Jackson. *Are they hiding out somewhere? Are they even alive? What is Ward planning?*

Dalton glanced out the window at the boarding house and noticed movement in one of the upstairs windows. A dark-complected man with black hair peered out at the post and telegraph office.

Since Billy is dead and Burkall is in custody, the man in the window has to be the fourth man, he decided. *But where had he come from? He had to have come up from the backside, down along the river. But why? Perhaps he had snuck Corrine and little Jackson into the hotel while his attention was on Ward.*

Looking over at Burkall, Dalton asked, "Is Corrine and my son in that boarding house?"

Burkall turned his head to Dalton, smiled, and shrugged his shoulders. Dalton decided the only way he was going to get information out of Burkall was to beat it out of him. But he didn't have time for that.

Dalton turned back to Daily. "Much obliged for your timely entrance. You the one been sendin' me those telegrams signed, '*a friend*'?"

"Yes, sir."

"Why the secrecy?"

"Well..." Daily began, as he glanced around, "in my line of work, it's best to keep a low profile."

Dalton thought about it a couple of seconds and said, "Yeah, I reckon that's so. Well, anyway, thank you for watchin' over Corrine and my son." Dalton glanced back out the window toward the hotel, then up and down the street as far as he could see. Looking back at Daily he asked, "Ya happen to know where my wife and child might be?"

"No, sir. No, I don't. I um... I was gonna make sure they got on the stage back to Fairbanks this morning," a frown crossed Daily's face, "but she gave me the slip and... well, by the time I figured out when and where, she was already halfway here."

Dalton looked back out at the upstairs window of the boarding house.

"One thing I learned about Corrine," he said, "don't underestimate 'er. When she gets a mind to do somethin', there ain't no stoppin' 'er. And she's generally right. I just wish I knew for sure if she's in that boarding house or not."

CHAPTER 17

DALTON WATCHED THE FRONT OF the boarding house and the upstairs window trying to formulate a plan. From his peripheral vision, he saw sudden movement to his right, down the street. Turning toward the movement, he saw Ted run across the street to the boarding house side.

"Son-of-a... Where's Ted going?" he demanded, looking around the room. Everyone looked at each other, then back at him. No one seemed to know.

Someone yelled from across the street. "Dalton. Dalton Laird. I know you're in there. My man upstairs saw ya. Evidently, Burkall got lost."

Laird looked back out the window toward the boarding house. Ward stood in front of the open door with his wide-brimmed hat pulled low, looking like he did when Dalton first met him back in the Amanita Saloon, eight years before.

Dalton opened the post and telegraph office door just enough to answer back. "No, Burkall ain't lost. He's sittin' here all nice and cozy by the fire."

Ward chuckled. "Knowin' you, I doubt he's cozy. I got something fer ya. Don't shoot…" Dalton looked out the door. "Here it comes."

Ward wound up like a baseball pitcher and flung something toward the door. It landed short but skittered on the hard-packed snow to the steps of the porch. It was Jackson's black wolf carving.

Dalton instantly felt a pain in his heart like it had been pierced by an arrow. Anger welled up and he gritted his teeth. Looking up at Ward across the street, and with a raised voice said, "Frank Ward, I should've killed you eight years ago. If you've harmed Corrine or my son…"

"They're alright. Fact is, I saved her and the kid's life out on the trail. Seems as though she ran into a mad moose. She's lucky I came along. Indian Charlie's got 'er and the kid tied up upstairs."

Dalton glanced at the upstairs window and saw Indian Charlie watching him behind a Winchester rifle.

"He's got instructions to cut 'em loose if you survive. If ya don't, you can rest assured I'll take care of 'er and the raise the boy as my own."

Dalton looked down at the floor and swore softly to himself. He couldn't be sure Corrine and Jackson were up there. *And where is Ted going?* He couldn't worry about that now.

Looking back at Ward, Dalton yelled, "Prove to me ya got 'er!"

Ward turned his head slightly toward the boarding house door and hollered, "Charlie, bring 'er to the window!"

Dalton watched Indian Charlie force a struggling figure to the window, backlit by lantern light. Dalton made eye contact with the figure and recognized his wife, Corrine. His eyes softened as he gazed at her, then grew hard and cold as he looked back at Ward.

"Just how do ya propose we handle this?" Dalton asked.

A smile crossed Ward's face. "Like the good old days, back in the states. We'll meet in the street in ten minutes. Just you and me."

* * *

Indian Charlie shoved Corrine back into the wooden chair, then returned to the window at the end of the room to watch the street.

Corrine's hands were tied behind her back and the rough rope chaffed at her wrists. Looking around the room, she saw that the upstairs bachelors' dormitory was one large room, lined with bunk beds against both long walls. In the center of the room, the downstairs stovepipe came through the floor and connected with the upstairs coal stove, then continued up through the roof. It stood between Corrine and the stairway. Charlie had seated them close to the stovepipe to provide her and Jackson with some warmth. Between the stovepipe and the stairway, stood a small table with a lit coal-oil lamp.

Jackson fussed, wanting Corrine to pick him up. "Sorry, son. I cannot do that," she told him. "My hands are tied."

"I untie them," he said, as he stepped behind her.

"No, I do not think you can, son."

Jackson pouted.

The thought occurred to her that it *would* give Jackson something to do to keep him busy. Besides, what if it worked and Jackson was able to loosen the knots? After all, Charlie hadn't tied them very tight, evidently in a show of respect for her.

"Alright, son. Show mommy you can to it."

As Jackson fiddled with the knotted rope, she felt it give a little. She smiled. Corrine caught a sudden movement in her peripheral vision at the stairway. Turning her head toward the movement, she saw someone looking into the room at floor level. It was Ted, the post office boy.

Corrine glanced at Indian Charlie then back at Ted, who by now was taking the last three steps up into the room. Corrine looked back at Charlie, concerned he would notice Ted, but evidently Charlie was more interested in what was happening on the street.

Ted stealthily made his way behind Corrine and knelt down, effectively hidden from Indian Charlie's view. But, as he did so, the floor squeaked and Jackson took a step back and said, "NO! I do it!"

Corrine felt the knot loosen even more and saw Charlie look in her direction.

"Hey. What..."

Corrine struggled to free her hands.

"Stop struggling, I'm trying—" Ted said.

"White mans, stop!" Charlie demanded, as he strode toward them with his rifle half-raised.

Corrine continued to struggle. She felt the knot loosen even more as Ted stood up to meet Indian Charlie.

Ted grabbed for Charlie. Charlie raised the rifle butt and smacked Ted upside the head.

Ted fell against the table and stove, knocking the coal oil lamp to the floor at the top of the stairs. It erupted in flames.

During the men's brief struggle, Corrine continued working the knot . Finally, the rope fell away. She reached up under her parka and pulled out White Moose's knife.

Indian Charlie made a grab for her.

Corrine drove the knife deep into Charlie's chest and pulled it back out.

Charlie dropped his rifle. Wide-eyed, he took a step backward and clutched his chest as he collapsed to the floor.

Corrine dropped the knife and picked up Jackson. Looking at the flames, she realized the stairway was blocked.

She suddenly realized *this* was the vision she'd had on the stage ride.

She let out a blood-curdling scream.

CHAPTER 18

DALTON DUG IN HIS PANTS' pocket and produced his Copenhagen, from which he took a dip. After replacing it in his pocket, he drew his 1911 and stepped out onto the porch. "Why wait?"

Ward threw a hasty shot. It buzzed past Dalton's head like an angry wasp and splintered the office doorpost. Dalton ducked. He returned a three-round burst as he ran down the porch and around the corner of the building. At that instant, Dalton heard Corrine scream. Quickly looking around the corner, Dalton saw all-at-once, flames dancing through the upstairs window and Ward turn and run into the boarding house.

Dalton bolted toward the boarding house, as well. His only thought was the safety of Corrine and little Jackson. But three steps into the street, Dalton lost his balance, stumbled, and fell on the hard-packed snow—his big toe throbbed with pain.

Regaining his stance, he pushed the pain aside. He half-limped and half-ran to the boarding house's porch.

Once inside the door, he moved to his left with his gun raised in a two-hand hold.

In the dim light of the interior, he could just make out Ted—his fire-singed hair smoking—leading a smoking, blanket-wrapped figure out of the flames and down the stairs.

He heard Jackson's cries coming from underneath the blanket.

Dalton knew it must be Corrine and his son. Ward stood at the foot of the stairs, his pistol pointed at Ted and reaching for Corrine. Dalton swung the 1911 at Ward and acquired his target.

Ward glanced back at Dalton. "Stop right there. One step closer and they die."

Ward yanked the blanket off Corrine and Jackson as they reached the bottom of the stairs. In one swift move, Ward pulled them around in front of him and held the gun to Corrine's head and side-kicked Ted in the stomach.

Ted stumbled back a couple of steps and fell over a chair, shattering it as he fell to the floor.

"Leave 'em be, Ward! They ain't part o' this!"

Little bits of smoldering embers floated down from the ceiling above their heads.

"Beg to differ with ya. She was mine before you came along," Ward said, the grin on his face more evil than happy.

Corrine turned her head toward Ward. "I was never yours," she growled.

Dalton noticed movement behind Ward. Ted stood up. The crackle and roar of the flames from the upstairs blaze covered any sound Ted might've made. Pieces of burning debris fell among the embers.

"Ward, I'm tellin' ya, let 'em go. You just said a minute ago ya wanted to do this the old fashion way. Out in the street. Just you and me."

Dalton watched Ted pick up a broken chair leg and start toward Ward.

Thought after thought seared Dalton's brain like lightning flashes in a heavy rainstorm.

Don't do it, Ted! You're gonna get yourself... Shoot! No! Don't have a clear shot! Damn!

Dalton helplessly watched as Ted gripped the chair leg like a baseball bat and got set to swing. The movement caught Ward's attention.

Turning his head and swinging his gun at the same time, Ward snapped a shot at Ted.

Ted went down.

Corrine, still holding Jackson in her left arm, spun to her left. She broke free of Ward's grip and raked her fingernails across his cheek.

She ran toward Dalton's right.

With a roar of rage, Ward swung his gun back toward Corrine. He fired a round that went wild.

NOW! Dalton's brain screamed as his trigger finger twitched.

Two rounds exited Dalton's 1911 so quickly it sounded like one.

Ward stumbled back a step then sank to his knees. He swayed there for a second, then looked down at his chest.

Dalton saw two red spots where Ward's heart used to be, so close together you could cover them with a silver dollar. Ward looked back at Dalton with a look of surprise on his face and then fell face-forward to the floor.

Dalton looked back and saw Corrine, still cradling Jackson, step out the door and onto the boardwalk. Satisfied they were safe, he turned his attention to Ted.

In the reddish glow of the firelight in the stairway, he saw Ted writhing on the floor, cupping his right shoulder. Dalton holstered the 1911.

"Ted? Ted, you all right?" Dalton asked, as he moved toward him. The roar and crackling of the fire overhead drowned out his words.

The charred, smoking ceiling just overhead suddenly burst into flames. Dalton involuntarily ducked as the heat and flames rolled across the ceiling toward the stairway, seeking a way up and out.

Reaching down, Dalton grabbed Ted by the collar with both hands and jerked him to his feet. He ignored the pain in his healing hands.

"Can ya walk?" Dalton yelled over the roar of the flames.

Ted nodded.

"Good! Let's get out of here!"

Dalton pushed Ted in front of him and guided him toward the front door.

A tremendous creaking and groaning from overhead resulted in a sudden crash. Dalton instantly realized the upstairs roof was caving in.

"Move it! Let's get out of here!"

The building shuddered in great spasms and the ceiling, above where they had been standing moments before, gave way. A tidal wave of sparks and heat and flame engulfed the first floor as Dalton shoved Ted out the front door and onto the boardwalk.

Moments later, Dalton, Corrine, Jackson, and Ted stood in front of the post and telegraph office. Looking back at the inferno raging across the street, they felt the paradoxical intense heat through the bitter cold of subarctic winter air.

Looking down, Dalton noticed the black wolf carving lying in the snow where Ward had thrown it earlier. The black paint reflected the fire, causing the toy to appear alive.

Picking it up, Dalton brushed the snow away. Turning to Corrine and Jackson he said, "Look what I found."

"*Zhoh Zhraįį.*" Jackson said, as he reached for his toy.

Dalton smiled and handed it to him.

"Thank you, Papa!"

Dalton's smile grew. He looked at Corrine and then at Jackson. "You're welcome, son."

Looking back at Corrine he asked, "You alright?"

Corrine smiled as a tear rolled down her cheek, then nodded that she was. Dalton embraced her and their son.

"Good. What'dya say we get off the street?"

CHAPTER 19

THE NEXT MORNING AS DALTON walked to the post and telegraph office, he saw stars shining through a partly cloudy sky, and it felt colder. Once there, he sent Marshal Brenneman a brief report of the previous day's events.

As he waited for the reply, he glanced out the window to the burned remains of the boarding house and the building next to it that had caught fire. Still smoldering in a heap, and somewhere in the middle of it, lay the remains of Frank Ward, Indian Charlie, and Billy Smith. Charles Daily had left earlier with his prisoner, Paul Burkall.

A few minutes later, Brenneman sent back a short telegram. It read:

WELL DONE. SEVERAL NEW DEPUTY MARSHALS COMING THIS SPRING.

YOUR SERVICES ARE NO LONGER NEEDED. THANK YOU.

Dalton smiled and thought, *It's about time.*

He took the badge off his chest and laid it on the counter. Turning to the telegraph operator, he said, "Mail this to the marshal's office in Fairbanks."

"Will do."

* * *

Dalton spent the next couple of hours rounding up the dogs that had been turned loose and put together two respectable teams of five dogs each. One for Corrine to drive, the other he had plans for. The rest of the dogs, Doc and his nurse could drive back to Nenana.

Walking into the hospital building, Dalton asked Doc, "Where is he?"

Doc nodded to one of the rooms.

Entering, Dalton saw Ted sitting up in the bed, the burns on his face and hands bandaged. Ted was looking out the window.

Ted turned his head toward Dalton and a smile crossed his face. "I thought you had left. Figured I wouldn't see ya 'til after Christmas."

Dalton smiled, closed the door and said, "We'll be leavin' in the mornin'." Then, walking over to Ted's bed he took a seat and said, "Couldn't leave ya without saying goodbye. You doin' alright?"

"Yeah, I'm alright. Just some minor burns and a scratch where the bullet nicked my shoulder. How's about Corrine an' little Jackson?"

"They're fine, thanks to you. Ya know, ya could've got yourself killed?"

Ted frowned, glanced around the room, then looked down at the blanket covering him as he said, "Yeah, but I told ya I would make it up to ya somehow."

A lump rose in Dalton's throat.

"I'm sorry, Ted. I shouldn't have got upset with ya about the telegram. It wasn't your fault."

"Aw, it's not just that," Ted began as he looked back at Dalton. "You were all alone against them four. Someone once told me that integrity is doin' the right thing even when no one is lookin' and you're all alone. Ya have a lot of integrity, Mr. Laird. But I didn't think it was right that ya had to do it all alone. I wanna be like you when I become a man."

Suddenly, the lump in Dalton's throat grew bigger and tears welled up in his eyes. Dalton reached up and cleared his vision with his sleeve.

"Ted, you're already a bigger man than most, and ya got more integrity than anyone I've met."

"Gee, ya really think so?"

"I know so."

Ted smiled then as Dalton stood up and picked up his parka. Turning back to Ted, Dalton said, "I want ya to come out to the Savage River cabin for the next couple of weeks and celebrate Christmas with us. Would ya like that?"

Ted's smile broadened into a grin, "Yes, sir. I sure would. I never really had a family to spend Christmas with." Then, a look of concern crossed Ted's face. "But, how will I get there?"

Dalton smiled at him.

"I put together a team of dogs for ya as a birthday present. Your boss said he'd help ya take care of them. Then, in a few days, when you're feelin' better, just follow the Stampede trail out of Lignite 'til you get to Savage River, then follow it upstream a coupla miles. Ya can't miss us. When ya get there, ya can help me build ya a cabin. Then ya can come and stay in it anytime ya like."

Dalton watched a tear roll down Ted's cheek and he felt the lump in his throat again.

"We'll see ya in a few days, alright?"

Ted smiled again and nodded his head.

* * *

Along about 2:30 p.m., just before sunset, Corrine and little Jackson brought Dalton a hot mug of coffee as he separated and sorted dog harnesses and ganglines in the dog yard. He removed one mitten and accepted it thankfully.

"I love you, Dalton Laird," she said. "I am sorry for doubting you and taking off to Nenana like I did. I... I caused you more trouble and worry by doing so."

Dalton put his arm around her. "I love you, too, Mrs. Laird. I'm just glad it all turned out alright."

"I am not sorry to see him gone," she began with a tone of disgust. "I hated that jacka—"

"Hey, watch your language!" Dalton smiled as he said it. "We have a youngun' among us. "

He took a sip of coffee. "It's clearin' up."

She looked up at him with questioning eyes. He nodded toward the sky. "The clouds. It's clearin' up and gettin' colder."

"PAPA! Look, Papa!"

"What is it, son?"

"Look!" Jackson said again, as he pointed to the south.

The air was deathly still. Little ice crystals twinkled in the air as all available moisture froze and slowly settled to earth. And there, through the twinkling crystals, he saw them.

Sun dogs.

Three suns just above the horizon, with an arc of light connecting the two outside suns.

"Well, look at that, would ya? That's the second one I've seen in four days. White Moose told me sun dogs in the evening means it's gonna be clear as a bell and cold as h—"

"Hey, watch your language!" Corrine admonished.

THE END

ABOUT THE AUTHOR

RUSSELL M. CHACE IS THE author of the Alaska historical fiction Dalton Laird series, which include books one and two—*From Out of The Loneliness* and *Under the Midnight Sun.*

As a teenager and young adult, he learned much of what he writes along the traplines and rivers he traveled by snowshoe, dog team and snow machine. It was during those years he wrote multiple articles for *Alaska Magazine*, *Fishing and Hunting News*, *Voice of the Trapper* and the *Alaskan Trapper*.

After moving to Colorado with his wife and two boys, Russell earned a degree in Criminal Justice and worked for the Colorado Department of Corrections for over twenty-two years. During that time, he was a member of the Emergency Response Team and the Escape Team, tracking escaped inmates in urban and suburban environments.

Russell is now retired and currently hard at work on his newest Alaska historical fiction novel. When not writing, he can be found fly-fishing, hunting, or prospecting the Arkansas River in the Rocky Mountains.